# THESE TWO HANDS

# These Two Hands

E. J. EDWARDS, S.V.D.

THE BRUCE PUBLISHING COMPANY
MILWAUKEE

98166

Imprimi potest: CAROLUS MICHEL, S.V.D., Superior Provincialis
Die 1 Augusti, 1942, Techny, Illinois
Nihil obstat: H. B. RIES, Censor librorum
Imprimatur: ✠ MOYSES E. KILEY, Archiepiscopus Milwaukiensis

Die 16 Octobris, 1942, Milwaukiae

DEDICATION

*To Those*
*Whose eyes shall see — the vision,*
  *of "the fields white for the harvest,"*

*Whose ears shall hear — the call,*
  *"Come, follow Me,"*

*And whose souls shall rise — to the sacrifice*
  *of leaving "father, mother, brother and*
  *sister for His Name's sake" —*

*To the missioners of the*
  *years to come.*

# Foreword

MANY Catholic layfolk seem to think that there is a dread monotony about all types of religious life. It appears to be an existence of cut-and-dried regulations whereby the individual is fitted into a mold. Shaped to an irrevocable design the Religious is vowed to a life of pious practices that ends with a routine burial.

Yet, there is another side to the picture, an especially human side. It is an aspect that will always be worth consideration as long as men of mortal frame dedicate themselves to the ideals of religious life. In subordinating self to the demands of any lofty ideal, the individual still remains an individual; his weaknesses are still with him, and his efforts to overcome them can yet retain the elements of human drama. The Religious in his moment of trial, in his struggles against himself, in his ultimate victory has not merely the stout staff of fellow Religious to lean upon, but also the strength of that mysterious élan, so potent to inspire, so enduring to assist, which we call Divine grace.

To most Catholics our foreign missioners are heroes; not in the sense of being heroes of military exploits, but rather as heroic plodders against lifelong obstacles of an alien language, of foreign customs, and of life in a far-off country. But that is not the whole truth. Our missioners are not supermen. They have human feelings, human weaknesses, and human emotions, just like the rest of us. Weak as their human hands may be for the trying task assigned to them, those same hands become heroically powerful when strengthened by the supernatural vigor of God's grace.

This is no mere figure of speech. In various ways God's grace comes palpably to all the foreign apostles. Seemingly the strangest and yet the commonest is through the very obstacles that beset them. Perhaps this is just another proof of the presence of Him who came not to destroy but to fulfill. The rock that obstructs becomes the foundation of the edifice; the fear that obsesses begets humility for exalted achievement; the people that appall become the teachers that uplift.

This does not detract from the heroism of our missioners. It is their own explanation for their achievements. In many ways they pass through a crucible of intensified trial. Frequently they are faced with situations that make a demand for mental grit as well as physical courage. The acts of martyrdom through which some of them have passed tell many a story of such heroism. Such acts are not formally recorded. There are many that will never be told.

In this book I try to tell one such story. I have set it down in the form of a tale in order that the vast army of the faithful may know and appreciate the fact that the fire which the Saviour lighted in men's hearts long ago is still with us: that even in our own day of vast strife the quiet flame of apostolic zeal may ignite the heart of Catholic youth, may inflame it to dare all, and may embolden it to conquer all — even itself.

# Contents

ix

# THESE TWO HANDS

# Prologue

THE beggar's eyes opened dully. Her tongue worked over the dried lips. She saw the young priest suddenly veer from her and go to the other side of the entrance. He dipped his fingers in the font of holy water and quickly blessed himself. Her cry *"Limos!"* (alms) died in her throat. This young missioner did not like her.

The morning moved slowly by on heat-dead feet. Outside, the tropic sun poured its fury of light and heat. The pool of shadow grew smaller and smaller. The light drew nearer the huddled beggar. She dozed in her filth and hunger. Again footsteps brought her awake. *"Limos!"* she croaked beseechingly.

Young Father Templeton stopped. He forced his eyes to meet those of the beggar, sitting in the penumbra of the shadow. A repulsive sight. Her rag of a skirt was huddled about her, one hand hidden in its folds. The unkempt greyish hair was drawn back of the head in a crude knot, which seemed to have been pulled so tight that the skin of the lower face was distorted by it. It gave a tight simian look to her features. The lower half of her eyelids puffed out bulbously like a frog's.

*"Limos!"* she cried again, and flapped one dirty, long hand up and down, palm upward.

He fumbled in his pockets vainly. "There is no money," he said in the dialect and turned away. His fingers still groping in his pockets found a hard metal object. He stopped and drew it forth. It was a religious medal. But maybe . . .

"*Medalle?*" he queried. "You care to have a medal?"

The beggar nodded. He drew near and dropped the medal in the outstretched hand. The mask of a face contorted in a smile, and the medal was pressed to her lips. The nauseous odor he had noticed on previous days, suddenly met his nostrils. He hastily walked from the entrance of the church into the glaring sunlight.

The church plaza was burnt brown. Little puffs of dust were scattered around his feet as he walked toward the large frame building on the farther side of the great square. His eyes lifted to the sign above it "Colegio de Sagrado Corazon." He was not thinking of the school. His mind was confused with the image of the filthy beggar and that nauseous smell. The conduct of this little Filipino school was entirely satisfactory to him. It was what he wanted: clean white cassocks, hours of class, afternoon siesta, shower, an hour of prayer each afternoon. This was suitable. The students were very naïve, nothing brilliant. But he lectured. Their response was not so very important. What was important was that he was among books.

But this wreck of a creature in the church vestibule disturbed him. She revolted and nauseated him. It did not seem right to let such creatures lie around in public. Yet, he was a priest. Kindness, charity, care for the poor . . . that was his calling. He felt he should do something, yet what? Repugnance was strong in him.

"Hey, Father Templeton!" called a voice.

He looked up. A square-shouldered, pallid-faced priest and a dapper Filipino layman stood in the doorway.

"Yes, Father Superior?" he replied.

"Is that beggar . . . that Luisa . . . in the church?"

"Yes. I just saw her."

Father Superior turned to the Filipino. "Come on, doctor."

Father Templeton laid a detaining hand on the Superior's arm. "Is anything wrong, Father?"

"Wrong? Oh . . . yes." He bethought himself of his manners. "This is Doctor Filomeno. He has come to take Luisa for a medical examination. It seems pretty sure she has leprosy."

The young priest watched the dust puffs squirt up from their footsteps as they strode across the plaza. "Leprosy!" He looked at his own right hand. That nauseous smell. He felt sick. Had he touched her when he gave the medal? He hastened to his room in search of soap and water.

2

The fly swooped into the porch. For a moment it rested on the hot white walls. Then it buzzed into the cool dark of the room and alighted on the neatly gathered-in mosquito net. There was no blistering sun here. It was pleasantly cool. The floor boards were dark and gleaming with wax. Serried bookshelves looked down on the white-cassocked figure at the desk. The fly swooped.

Irritably Father Templeton brushed at the intruder. Why didn't they put screens on the windows? His eyes lifted to the expanse of the open veranda. They had told him the typhoons blew screens in and that the rainy season rusted everything but copper. He sighed. *"Mañana land,"* he muttered, and turned back to his task of correcting papers.

A hasty knock disturbed him. "Yes?" he called out.

The houseboy came in hastily. "Faddaire . . . tha-a-t one . . . tha-a-t Luisa is dying."

"Luisa?" His pencil fell to the desk. Father Superior had been taking care of her since she had been segregated; he was in charge of all the parish work anyhow. "Isn't Father Superior here?" he asked.

"No; he hab a call in the barrio."

A curious feeling stole over the priest. Anoint that leper? Put his hand to that tainted flesh? A cold qualm shook him again. He heard his voice saying: "When will Father Superior come back?"

"Maybe half hour. Maybe one hour."

"Half hour?" His hand fumbled and found the pencil. "I've got to finish these papers. Tell Father Superior as soon as he comes in, eh? He will take the call."

The boy went out, slowly, quietly, as though rebuked for his hasty and unnecessary entrance. Father Templeton sat immobile. The fly buzzed about him. Seizing a sheaf of papers he smashed it out of existence. As though relieved by this display, he settled down to the work before him. For more than an hour he worked steadily through the papers, making his corrections and assigning the percentages in a neat scholarly hand. He liked the tidiness of his own handwriting.

A door banged on the floor below. Father Superior had returned. A few moments later the door banged again;

obviously the Superior had taken the call. The priest sighed and stood up. He took his breviary and went to the church.

## 3

Slowly Father Templeton mounted to his room. It had been a very uneasy hour. He had never known that prayer could be so tasteless, so much a burden. What was it? His mind had been upset by that unexpected call. Parish work and schoolwork . . . they did not mix. One needed quiet, regularity, and peace for the latter. A professor's schedule had no place for sick calls and the sudden demands of soul care. Unless, of course, in cases of grave emergency. Epidemics, for instance. But in the year he had spent at the task of teaching, there never had been any such intrusions on his well-ordered life. He was thankful that someone else had taken that sick call.

He opened the door of his room. Someone had lit the lamp; its cone of mellow radiance disclosed a figure in the chair at his desk. He glanced at the papers in its hands. The papers he had been correcting.

"Father Superior?" he faltered "Were you . . . were you looking over my work?"

The Superior's face showed white. "Are these what you were working on, Father, when that sick call came?" he asked in a tight voice. His hand held up the sheaf of papers.

"Yes, Father Superior."

The Superior's lips tightened and a ridge appeared along his jaw. Slowly and coldly, like pellets of stone in a still pool of water the words came. "Do you think these papers are worth more than a soul?"

Before the young priest could answer, the papers went crashing into the wastebasket. The Superior rose from the chair and stood erect. His eyes met the wide-staring ones of the young priest. "Yes," he said, "Luisa died . . . before I got to her."

Across the desk the two men looked at each other in silence. The Superior seemed to be awaiting some apology, some excuse, from the younger priest.

Father Templeton hung his head. He had no answer ready. It was not the correction of the papers that had held him from taking that sick call. No, he knew it was something else, something he dared not voice. He saw clearly, now when it was too late, that he had been afraid. How could he tell that to the Superior? He lifted his eyes, and the Superior's searching glance saw the truth as plainly as if the words had been spoken.

"So that was it, Father? You were afraid."

By way of reply, the young priest hung his head.

"Let me tell you something, young man," the quiet voice was under control but was as sharp as a knife. "All our missioners have failings. Some are impetuous, others are untidy and cannot seem to be able to keep order either in their own lives or in those of others, and most of us are narrow. Yes, Father, we all have our faults. But we are priests." Then the voice rose into something like a shout. "Do I have to tell you that when a soul calls for you there is only one thing to do? Do I have to explain to you that a call from a dying person comes before every-thing else? Don't you realize that?"

The outraged and accusing figure at last drew from

the young priest the very last thing he wanted to say. "I was not on duty, Father Superior."

"What? You, a priest, dare to say that! Not on duty! Why, man, when a soul is dying, you have no other duty. That is a duty that no priest shirks. You are the first to show that failing around here. Afraid! You, a priest, a missioner, afraid to administer the sacraments to a dying woman! And then you say that you were not on duty! Twenty-three years on the missions and I never met anything like it before! Am I dreaming all this?"

For a moment longer the tension lasted. Then the Father Superior turned his back on the young priest and looked out into the darkness of the plaza. For a long period of time — it might have been a minute or it might have been an hour, but it seemed like an eternity to Father Templeton — the tall trim figure stood between the desk and the window. Then the Superior said, without turning toward the young priest: "I shall see you in my office in fifteen minutes, Father." A moment later he had left the room.

When Father Templeton entered the Superior's office, all traces of excitement had disappeared from the older man's demeanor. There was no longer the accusing fire in the man's eyes, no longer the biting words on his lips. He even motioned the young priest to a chair by the side of the desk. Father Templeton thought this a sign of a paternal lecture. He prepared himself to hear the worst, but what the Superior said was beyond anything he had feared.

"Father Templeton, you will leave Minandang. I am appointing you to the station at Santa Cruz. The boat leaves day after tomorrow. Have your things ready by eight o'clock on Thursday morning. Is that clear, Father?"

"I'll be ready, Father," was the reply. There was nothing of petulance or sulkiness about the voice. He had not quite expected his punishment to take this form, and he knew he would miss the peace and quietness of the school life. But he was ready to take his medicine. At least, with God's help he was ready. He hoped that the life on a lonely mission station like Santa Cruz would not be too terrible.

"All right, Father Templeton, that's all. I'll see you before you go."

# FUTILITY:

"We have toiled all night and have taken nothing" (*Peter to Christ*).

# Chapter I

FATHER BUFF CONNERS lay back indolently in the *mañana* chair. A breeze from the bay wafted across the veranda, cooling, restful. The thick muscular hands of the priest rested idly on his knees. The last three fingers of the left hand stood out stiffly over the curve of the knee; they had been broken years ago and had not been reset properly, but the accident did not seem to have weakened the powerful hand. Even in repose, the priest was the picture of strength. His shoulders were big and husky, his chest was like a barrel, and an unusually large head with close-cropped grey hair accentuated the impression of hugeness. If it were not for a pair of light blue eyes and a mouth that was shaped to laughter, you might have thought that this Father James Conners was too husky for other people's good. But among his brother missioners he was loved for his gentleness as much as for his ready sympathy.

In his young days in the Islands he had run his head against so many traditions that he had sometimes hurt himself. He always wanted to get things done and was impatient of delays. So some young priest had once called him Buff because he buffaloed his way through all kinds of obstacles. The name had stuck. Officially he was Father James Anthony Conners, but the brethren had long ago chosen to forget his baptismal names. To every priest in the Islands he was Father Buff Conners, a wailing wall in time of distress and a font of wisdom in days of trouble.

Just now he was listening to his young neighbor at the station of Santa Cruz, Father Francis Templeton. The boy was unhappy, and Father Conners had run over to visit him, knowing that there must be a reason for the unhappiness. Besides, while Father Templeton was obviously an excellent priest and had a good scholastic record, he didn't seem to be doing any great work at Santa Cruz. What was the matter with the youngster?

"Suppose, Frank," he said quietly, "you tell me just what it was that happened at Minandang." He threw up his hand as the other lifted his head. "Yes, yes, I had news of it by letter. What I want is your account. You're in a bad way, Frank. I'd like to be of help if I can."

The young missioner looked into the heavy-featured countenance. The older man waited.

"I am sure of that, Buff," Father Templeton replied, after a long pause. "You see, I've always been keen on books. Perhaps it has made me a hopeless idealist. I volunteered for the foreign missions. It never struck me that it would be like . . . it is out here." He hesitated. "It made me glad," he continued, "when they appointed me to schoolwork at Minandang and not to a mission station."

"Yes?" encouraged the other.

"You know the setup at Minandang."

The elder priest nodded and Father Templeton slid his tongue over dry lips. "One afternoon a sick call came."

"Uh-huh," grunted his listener understandingly.

Haltingly, shamefacedly the story was told. At its conclusion the brown eyes looked into the wide open blue ones. "By a sort of grapevine, within an hour everyone knew what I had done. I began to feel the unspoken criticism of the brethren. It was only two days, but they were more than two days. They were uncounted hours and minutes and seconds of hopeless misery. You see, Buff, I was unable to justify myself, even to myself. It's an awful thing for a priest to realize that he is a coward. Well, I couldn't do anything about it. But I could take my medicine. It was a relief to get shipped out here to one of the remotest spots on the island. At least I am away from that sense of everyone accusing me."

"You like it here then?"

"No, I don't. I certainly don't. But I can be alone, and I . . . . I sort of feel that I want to be alone and think."

"Think?" snorted Father Conners. "That's just what you don't want to do. What you want to do is work."

"There's not much of that to be done in this little fishing village, Buff," replied the other a bit wearily. "I say Mass for them. They come on Sundays, of course. They are not interested in anything else."

Father Conners looked as if he had a lot of things to say to this. But he asked instead: "What did the Superior say to you?"

"Not much. Simply that I was appointed to the station at Santa Cruz. I've been here long enough. I don't fit."

"Don't fit, what do you mean, Frank? Try the life before you quit it."

"I have, Buff. It is plain that the Superior himself is convinced I don't belong. He just wants me to spend some time here before I go home, so that it will not appear as though I am being expelled for this misdeed of mine."

"Tripe!" was Father Conners' sudden and succinct comment. "I know the Superior. He is giving you a chance to come back, to redeem yourself."

Father Templeton flashed a startled glance at the older priest. "You mean, this is to be sort of a test?"

"Sure."

"Another chance," mused Father Templeton half aloud, "that is just what I have been thinking about these past weeks. It's what hurts. You see, Buff, it is almost a certainty with me that if the same occasion arose, I would act in the same way. You see, I'm sort of . . . well, made that way."

"In other words, you're afraid."

"I guess I am," admitted the other wearily. Father Conners stood up and walked to the rail of the veranda. The bay spread out before him, glorious in the afternoon's tropic sun. He had no eyes for the beauty of it all. He was thinking. When he faced about, it was to see a very dejected young man with his face buried in his hands.

"Lift up your head a minute, Frank," he said, not unkindly. "I am about to unload the vials of my theology upon you. Before I do so, let me tell you I'm a rather pig-headed sort of person now. They call me the Buffalo. I wasn't quite such a determined man in my first years. Many a time my knees got wobbly. I read up on this thing called fear and labored over it in my own way. The language may be that of Buff, but the voice is that of St. Thomas."

Slowly the young priest's head came up. Encouraged,

Father Conners sat on the edge of his *mañana* chair. "When we know what a thing is about, Frank, we've got it half licked. Fear means you want to run away from some evil which you think you can't beat." He paused. Father Templeton did not appear deeply interested. Unperturbed, Buff continued. "Now, in your case, you welshed on a call of duty because of the repulsiveness of the woman's disease. The realization that if you met the same condition you would act the same appalls you. You are scared stiff. Am I right?"

"You are, Father," agreed the other. "And how am I to know if this cowardly streak extends to one particular thing. Suppose I shirk all the other difficulties too, sickness, physical hardships, contact with the people?" He stopped abruptly.

"Does the notion of these things also bother you?" probed Father Conners.

It was some moments before the answer came. "Yes. I've given it a great deal of thought these past weeks. I'm afraid to attempt anything for fear I'll discover just how far-reaching this . . . cowardice is."

Buff stood up and walked abruptly to the railing of the veranda again. His arms, in a characteristic pose, were held slightly out from his sides, as though ready to make a tackle. Without turning he said: "Did you ever fear fear?"

"Fear fear?" repeated Father Templeton.

"That's what I said," replied the other curtly. "You're thinking too much. You can stretch this terror business indefinitely. Fear has to be repelled. You've got to do more and think less."

"Do what, Buff?" pleaded the young priest.

Father Conners went up to him. "Look, Frank, not so very long ago you had a brave dream of saving souls. The practical aspect of it never crossed your mind. Souls don't drop into your lap like ripe apples from a tree. It takes grim tenacity, sweat, tears, courage to get them. You've got to battle the devil, the world, and . . . yourself." He paused and let his hand come down on Father Templeton's shoulder. "Your first time at bat, you struck out. Are you going to quit completely because of that? You weren't fit for the job . . . practically. I suppose mentally, spiritually, you are miles above the rest of us. You've got to build up the other side of yourself. You've got to toughen yourself to meet life as it is. You must face its disagreeable side in order to make your dreams come true. They can, you know."

Father Conners went over and sat in his chair, his eyes on the dejected figure in front of him. For more than a minute that figure never moved; then the young priest seemed to have arrived at some decision.

"Just tell me what I must do first."

"Go among the people."

"But how is that going to help?"

"I'll not answer that now. Just trust me."

A long pause. Then the young priest's eyes looked deeply into those of his companion. "I will, Buff."

"But I'm not through yet, Frank. Listen to me a moment. I know you think at present that you are entirely out of your class, superior to them." Father Templeton colored. The shot had gone home. "You are," Buff hastened to add, "in some respects. We all come out here to teach these people wisdom. Wisdom is manifold. The exchange is not one-sided."

"Faddaire!"

A small boy stood at the entrance to the veranda.

"Yes, Totoy?" replied Father Templeton.

"The boat is ready now for the Faddaire."

"Gosh! Is it that late already?" ejaculated Father Conners. "All right, Totoy, tell them I'll be right along."

The boy vanished. Father Templeton arose. "I hate to see you go, Buff. This talk has helped me a lot."

"Glad of that, Frank," replied the other. "There is just one other thing. If a missioner doesn't have fear of some sort or other, it's a bad sign."

"You're not just saying that to be encouraging?"

"No; just truthful. Love is the thing that prepares us for fear. A great love — a great fear. With every love there is the fear of losing what is loved. You love the missionary ideal, you fear the least shortcoming in the carrying out of it."

Father Templeton's eyes lit up at this thought. His companion's face broke out into a grin. "That's a lot better," he applauded. "You are far from home, but you are not exactly solo. I'll drop down to see you as often as I can. And . . . there's always Someone in the church who can help."

"I know that," replied the other simply. "I haven't been merely thinking these past weeks. I have been praying."

"That's the right line. Prayer taps a divine reservoir. Doesn't that give you hope? Sure. And hope kicks the pants off of any fear."

They took their sun helmets and left Father Templeton's small convento. Down the sands of the shore they walked: two figures in flowing white cassocks.

For a long time Father Templeton watched the *banca* cleaving the waters of the bay until it rounded the headland and was lost to sight. When he walked back to the convento, there seemed to be a new spring in his step, a strange lightness in his heart.

## 2

**Rising** mountainously from the sea, the Island of Piloan is a day's journey south of Manila. It lies like a long finger in the sapphire swells of the South China Sea. Minandang, the capital town, is far up the northwest coast. There are no roads. Innumerable bays and coves cut into the shoreline. High volcanic mountains ridge the island and make direct communication from east to west coast impossible. A small steamer, tramping from one town to another and then back to Manila, keeps the towns in contact with the outer world. Santa Cruz Bay, on whose shore nestled the fishing village of Father Templeton, was on the southmost tip of Piloan. Two huge arms of mountains ran westward from the shore and reached down into the sea, forming a vast attempt to close in on the waters. Thither came the interisland steamer every Tuesday and Father Templeton had chosen it for the initial attempt at carrying out Father Conners' advice.

"Go among the people?" It had not been an auspicious start. He strode hastily down the dusty lane lined with shabby shacks. *Tiendas,* they were called. His sidewise glances took in the open fronts with their medley of cheap wares. Fishing equipment, cheap Japanese cloth, *sari-sari tiendas* with their potpourri of oriental minutiae, a rice *tienda,* a *halo-halo* stand. Sloppy Chinos, hollow-chested, clad in white shorts and cotton undershirts, clacked forward on their wooden *chinelas* to gaze blandly at him.

The sun was hot overhead. Smells from fish and copra intermingled. A scabrous mongrel, disturbed in its sleep by his passing, stood up slowly, bared its teeth, turned slowly around, and again lay down in the dust of the road.

Totoy had to double his steps to keep up with the hurried pace of the priest. They left the cluster of ill-smelling *tiendas.* The path became a road the width of a carabao cart. It was rough, made up of crushed white corals. Totoy looked up at the clean-shaven jaw and firm thin lips beneath the helmet. The Padre was silent; his cheeks flushed, his eyes fastened on the ground.

"It is hot, Faddaire," ventured the boy.

"Yes . . . it is 'Toy," agreed the priest abstractedly. Regal palms now lined the road. Their shade was welcome. A line of women passed, carrying effortlessly on their heads large wicker trays filled with fish. They stared silently at the white-gowned figure as they went by. Their remarks, a gurgle of laughter, after they had gone past him came to his ears. Father Templeton bit his lower lip. What did they think him? A freak?

"You are tired, Faddaire?" said Totoy's voice at his elbow.

"Tired? No. I haven't done anything to get tired."

"But your head is down."

Unconsciously the priest jerked the offending member upright. "Oh . . . that! That was because I was thinking."

He fell silent again but inwardly he was upbraiding himself. Couldn't he at least look at a thing before he ran
from it? The palms at the left side of the road were more
dense. He could no longer catch a glimpse of the bay
through them. A lumbering train of carabao carts plodded
past. Huge, long, green bamboos were lashed to them,
their farthermost tips whipping up and down with the
movement of the cart. Other carts followed bearing clus-
ters of bananas, baskets of mangoes lusciously gold, the
small round chicos with their rough brown surfaces,
langanissa, durians, and a host of other fruits that were
yet foreign to him. "That is for the boat to take to
Manila," explained Totoy.

"Uh-huh," grunted the priest unappreciatively.

"It is from the hacienda."

"Hacienda? What hacienda?"

"The hacienda of Don Ernesto," elaborated the boy.
"Up there," his vague gesture took in the mountains in
general.

The priest was not interested.

"You know that, Faddaire?" questioned Totoy.

"What?"

"Th - a - a - t." Father Templeton's gaze followed the
boy's finger. A youngster trundled a curious conveyance
toward them. To a short bamboo pole was attached a
wooden wheel. The pole rested on the boy's shoulder, the
wheel on the ground. Midway along the pole hung a tin
can. The boy's two hands rested on the pole and he pushed
it blithely ahead of him.

"He will get water," explained Totoy. "It is easier than
to carry the pail."

The water carrier passed in silence.

" 'Toy," exclaimed the priest, "did you know that boy?"
"Yes, Faddaire."

"Why didn't you say hello?"

"I did, Faddaire. Like this." Totoy pointed to his eyebrows which he suddenly lifted and dropped again. "That is our Filipino way," he grinned.

They continued along the road. The priest's desire was to reach the end of it where it debouched into a square of moth-eaten grass in front of his church and convento.

"The letter, Faddaire?" asked Totoy shyly.

"The letter?" said the priest blankly.

"Is it from America?"

"Oh, the letter, yes," said Father Templeton. He had utterly forgotten that he had had a letter this morning. It was still clasped in his hand. He glanced at it. "No; it's from Minandang." He tore it open and read as they walked. Gradually his pace slackened. He came to a dead halt. Totoy stopped and fixed his gaze interrogatively on the priest. "It's nothing, 'Toy. The Father at Minandang wants me to get corals for the school collection. Where can I get them?"

The boy's reply was prompt. "We will ask that Lacay (old man) Luis."

"And where is he?"

"We can find him now under the buri palm," said the boy confidently.

"How do you know?"

"He always sits there, every day, at this time."

"And where is the buri palm?"

"I will show you, Faddaire."

A bypath turned left from the road and entered the

thick clustering cocoanut palms. As they followed the
path, the number of nipa hunts increased till they came
to a spot where another path intersected. Here a perfect
tangle of huts took up all the available space beneath
the trees.

"This is where all the people live, Faddaire," said Totoy.
"That other place," with a gesture toward the *tiendas*
and pier, "is the *mercado* (market place)."

Soon the sea showed through the trees. The road
brought them right to the beach. The last tree was a giant
buri palm, its spiked frond casting a wide area of shade
on the soft sands.

"Adios!" exclaimed the boy. "He is not here."

Some people were approaching. "Never mind, 'Toy,"
the priest hastened to answer. "We can see him later.
Can we get to the convento by walking along the beach,
or do we have to go back to the road?"

"It is the same, Faddaire."

They went along the beach. When they arrived at the
convento Totoy said: "He will be there tonight, Faddaire, sure. He will tell stories."

"All right then. We will see him tonight."


3


The creamy light of a tropical moon flooded the bay.
A gentle wind quivered over the waters. Great blobs of
shadow loomed beneath the palms. The stillness was so
soft that it almost seemed to breathe.

In the light of the moon, a circle of figures squatted on
the sand. Many had cloths tied about their heads. They

feared to become moonstruck. Behind them was the dark curtain of the nipa huts and the palms; before them, the sea lovely in its stillness. But they had no eyes for these things. Lacay Luis had them in thrall. His voice was pleasant, with frequent dramatic pauses. He had a trick of monotoning the last part of a sentence that gave it a certain solemnity. Hidden in the shadows Father Templeton and Totoy listened.

"Visayas, we call them, those six beautiful islands to the south of us," said the old man. "Why they are called Visayas is an old story. Formerly they were six dark-eyed princesses, the daughters of the Sun and the Moon. They lived on one vast verdant island. Loving sisters were these beautiful girls and they ruled in peace and perfect concord. High above them the Sun by day, and the Moon by night, gazed pridefully at the affection and union that made their children live so happily." The old man stretched out an arm toward the bay. "The sea is change-able, is it not? Tonight it is gentle, a lamb. Tomorrow it is terrible, a tiger. There came a day when the love of the six daughters changed to hate. They became divided. Each took a portion of the island and ruled it as queen. They would have nothing more to do with each other.

"Their father, the Sun, saw this and was filled with anger. He resolved to punish them. The sky split with blue lightning, the thunder rolled like war drums, by day and night the rains fell and howling winds blew.

"The Moon, mother of these six discontented daughters, was incensed too and desired their punishment to be long drawn out and severe. But her motherly heart could not disregard the cries of her stricken children. The rain beat down upon them; the thunder frightened them with its deafening roar, the lightning blinded them; the wind and water lashed them helplessly about. The Moon-mother begged the Sun-father to relent, to pity the distress of their children. But the Sun paid no heed. Instead he called aloud to his stricken daughters: 'You desired to rule alone . . . you shall do so!' Then the earth shook to its foundations. Huge fissures ran through the island's length and breadth and the greedy waters of the deep rushed in.

"That night the Moon-mother came to mourn over the desolation. Amazed, she saw a fairy picture. Instead of the one large island, six islands lay lovely in the moonlight. She could see the hills and mountains, the verdant forests, the splashing waterfalls, the salt-white strand. And there on each beautiful island sat a beautiful but disconsolate daughter of hers. Bitter tears they wept, for now they were separated indeed."

The old man paused and gazed around his circle of listeners. "For that reason," he explained, "we call these islands the Visayas. *VI* means six; and *sayas* in their dialect means skirts. The six skirts of the six beautiful daughters of the Sun." He appended a moral — "They could not live in peace."

The story was ended. Some stood up and told him how they had enjoyed it. Lacay Luis liked to hear commendations. This had been his hour. For a brief period of time he reigned supreme. Others listened. He could make them laugh or cry, make them eager or indignant. To him it was like playing an instrument. His hearers' hearts were his instrument, and as he narrated a tale his eyes kept flickering from one face to another, catching, gauging the response.

His own face was not exactly a thing of beauty. To Father Templeton, it seemed a skein of deep folds and innumerable wrinkles. Beneath the large upper lip a wad of betel nut reposed, giving it a puffed appearance. His hair was brush-cropped in true fisherman tradition, but it was thin and of a dirty grey. The moonlight accentuated the hollows at his temples and beneath his collar bone. The priest had been advised by Totoy of the old man's owlish trick of drooping both lids over his eyes instead of saying yes. As the priest stood before him now he received the impression of something ancient and wise, of vast simplicity and profound adroitness. The old man's eyes lifted. There was no movement of surprise. "Apo," he said. It was a greeting and a welcome.

The priest's heart rose. At least here was one that was aware of his existence.

"Apo," he greeted back and hunkered down in the sand.

Totoy explained the Padre's need. The old man's reply was instantly forthcoming. "Ramon will take you tomorrow. I shall tell him. There is a coral reef there," his bony finger pointed to the bay as readily as though it were the page of a book. "It has many beautiful corals. You can swim, Apo?"

"Yes, Lacay Luis."

"You will enjoy it."

They chatted a while, and then the priest and the boy left.

"How old is Lacay Luis?" asked the priest as they padded through the soft sand.

"No one knows, Faddaire. Very old that one. But he is a berry fine storyteller."

Father Templeton probed further and discovered that not only was the old man an able raconteur, but also a very enthusiastic one, and that in the wholeheartedness of his narration he was prone to mix fact and fable. So much so that the simple folk thought he was giving the statement of an eyewitness when he told the story of creation. An old line came to the priest's mind and he rashly ticketed Lacay Luis with it: "Old men — more tongue to them than truth."

# Chapter II

It WAS midmorning. The scythe-nosed *banca* sliced a furrow through the bright blue waters. Buoyant as a floating gull, it slipped smoothly over the waters of the bay. Seated in the center of the *banca*, the priest visioned the boat as the spirit of man winging its way over the world's wide expanse. The vast sky arched above, the horizon limitless before him, and all about him the glorious gold of the sun-smitten sea. A cockleshell, rising, falling, but ever thrusting forward through the waves — the spirit of man.

The priest's thoughts were interrupted by the sound of notes being plucked from a guitar. He turned to look at the guitarist, but Ramon only laughed. The boy could do tricks with his voice, and he was giving the new priest an exhibition of his imitation of a man playing a guitar. Then he began to sing one of the Island songs. His voice had a deep vibrant quality, full of overtones. The priest had not met him before; and he marvelled now at the carefree happiness in the boy's face. It was not quite the face of a Filipino. Instead of being dark, the skin was of a golden-bronze hue. The eyes were alert and fearless, and the face was crowned with a head of thick black hair which had a pronounced wave in it. Quite a picture, the priest thought, as he looked at the supple-muscled, lithe, and hardy body, and listened to the boy's song.

Suddenly the singing ceased. Ramon shouted and from his position in the rear of the *banca* pulled a rope. The sail rattled down and with it the priest's poetic fancies. Totoy scrambled forward and secured the sail.

"Is this the place?" asked Father Templeton.

For reply, Ramon pointed to the water. "Look, Padre!"

Father Templeton peered over the side of the *banca*. "Wait, Padre," ordered Ramon, "put these on and put your face in the water." The priest affixed a pair of goggles, a stout rubber band holding them to his head. Ramon, equipped in similar fashion, slid his supple body over the side of the *banca*. The priest joined him, holding fast to the front bar of the outrigger. After the hot sun, the water was deliciously refreshing. They plunged their faces beneath the water. A world of wondrous beauty opened to them. It was a reef, a fairyland of colours. They withdrew their heads from the water.

"You see what you want, Padre?" asked Ramon.

"More than that," exclaimed the priest. "Let's go."

It was not very deep. They released their hold on the outrigger and dove. The world suddenly changed. A delicate blue-green arras was all about them. Out of fluttering shadows reared pink and orange growths — living corals. A sea plume, royal purple in colour, swayed gently like a fern in a soft breeze. A flurry of gorgeously tinted rainbow fish fled before them. Into the priest's path drifted a large loose fluff of fairy lace that looked like the most delicate of chiffons. The priest was about to touch it when Ramon's hand pushed him hard. They shot to the surface. "That lace?" gasped the priest. "Jellyfish," was Ramon's succinct explanation. "Very painful if you touch. Like a burn."

Father Templeton told him the types of coral he wanted. Ramon plunged and brought them up, one at a time, while Totoy kept the boat in position. The priest clung quietly to the outrigger. He had a keen appreciation of nature's beauties and for the moment his mind was bewildered. His eyes had had such a surfeit of colours. It needed some moments of readjustment before going back to it. He inhaled deeply and dove. Gaudy parrot fish, schools of silvery moonfish idled by. His hand touched sand of startling snow-white colour. All about it were strewn starfish — sepia, mauve, crimson — a tapestry of colour. His glance fell upon a glorious cluster of gorgonias, their coloring a rich oxidized purple. Hastily he kicked his way to the top. He trod water over the spot till Ramon appeared. Clinging to the outrigger, he watched absorbedly as Ramon brought up his treasures.

"You like this, Faddaire?" queried Totoy.

"Huh? — Oh, you bet, 'Toy. It's great. Wish I could hold my breath longer under water. Like Ramon. I see only a bit of all that wonderland and then I've got to bounce up again for air. Well, here goes again."

Each ensuing dive opened up new wonders. Coral castles, greyish violet fonts of sponges, moonlike blobs of jellyfish, swarms of tiny fish streaking past like little comets. Vases of sheer violet, giant ferns undulating ever so gently, chrysanthemums frosted over with a mist of shining crystals. It was like a fairy world.

Ramon finally climbed into the boat and Totoy eagerly donned his goggles. Father Templeton, still in the water, hung on to the side of the *banca* and gazed at the heaps of treasure they had amassed. Colours — pearl-grey, onion-skin pink, luscious salmon. But they had looked so much prettier beneath the water. Now they seemed to have lost their pastel shades in the glaring light of the sun.

"You are a good swimmer, Padre," commended Ramon quietly.

The priest looked at him. He sat like a young god. Bronzed, sea water dripping from his tousled black hair, red rims about his eyes where the goggles had pressed, his bolo at his side. The priest grinned. "A long way from being as good as you, 'Mon."

Ramon beamed. Totoy stood up. "I will be the one to get you the last coral, Faddaire," declared the boy.

"All right, chico," agreed the priest laughingly.

With a splash Totoy hit the water and disappeared from view.

"Think I'll go after him," said the priest, "and see what he gets."

He submerged. The boy swam swiftly ahead of him down to the reef's floor. Before a cavern of buff-colored coral he stopped. His hands began to tug at something embedded in the sand. Behind him, Father Templeton felt tired, in need of a breath. He pushed hard on the floor of the reef with his feet and shot upward. His heart suddenly turned to ice. Flashing upward, a terrifying sight seared his eyes. Two fiery, lynx eyes, with white rims, a thick circular lip and a great parrotlike beak leered out of the dark. It seemed the essence of all evil issuing out of the dim night of the coral cavern. A tentacle waved sinuously over Totoy's unsuspecting back. How he got to the surface, Father Templeton never could relate. He was kicking with all his might, but he scarce seemed to move. His head struck the outrigger. With one sweep he tore the goggles from his head. " 'Mon! 'Mon!" he shrieked as his hand punched the water. "Quick! Quick! 'Toy—"

Ramon's lithe body cut the water like a knife. In a frenzy of fear the priest thrashed over to the boat and pulled himself aboard. He peered over the side, his breath coming in great shuddering gasps. Wildly he thrust his face into the water. A coal-black cloud suddenly blossomed out of the depths below. Trembling violently, he lifted his face and gulped some air. He looked again. The cloud was spreading its sepia stain. A pair of legs flashed. Ramon was clear. Two heads bobbed up. Ramon scrambled aboard and dragged Totoy in. Speechless and weak, the priest gazed at them. A sudden pain in his foot broke the spell. He was standing on a coral. His foot was bleeding. Dazedly he stepped aside and sat down. Ramon turned the limp boy over. A flat, slatey-grey, bladelike thing adhered to the youngster's shoulder. Ramon went to work on it with the tip of his bolo. "This is piece of the devilfish, Padre," he explained. "There are suckers on this. When it touches the skin it makes a blister. Two months before it is healed."

"How — how are you, 'Toy?" asked the priest anxiously.

The boy was gulping and trying to vomit. He brought up some water.

"He swallowed water when the devilfish touched him," said Ramon. "He is not hurt."

Totoy managed a bedraggled sort of smile to prove it and sat up.

Ramon pointed his bolo to the black cloud that clung like a fungus to the water. "The devilfish is defeated," he stated proudly.

The priest looked and shivered. The tropical sun was beating down on his bare back but he did not sense its warmth. His breath came with difficulty and his heart seemed pumping ice water.

As Ramon paddled home he explained to an enthralled Totoy how he had thrust his thumbs into the eyes of the devilfish, blinding it and then had slashed the one tentacle that had laid hold of him. The inky cloud was the devilfish's confession of defeat and he had moaned and cried and withdrawn while they fled. Father Templeton heard Ramon's voice as if at a distance. His eyes were fixed in a stare upon the heaped-up corals all about the bottom of the *banca*. They had no longer any beauty in his eyes. He realized that he had been cowardly, terribly so, and that the fear was even now upon him. He had failed again and it had almost cost a life. Shame and confusion poured over him.

He looked up with a start. They were at the shore. He stumbled out of the boat. Totoy was showing the blistered spots on his shoulder. Ramon was explaining to a group of fishermen why he had not been able to kill the devilfish and bring it home to eat. Lacay Luis approached slowly and inspected the corals. He turned to Ramon. "Ay, 'Mon," he said, "close to the fire you are easily warmed." The men laughed. The priest looked blank. "He means, Padre," explained Ramon, "that I found the corals at the place he told me."

The priest made no answer. No one seemed to be particularly upset. Did they not realize how close they had been to tragedy, to death? Bewildered, he made for the convento.

# Chapter III

T HE man's figure was a disgrace for a fisherman to view: squat little body with a bulbous protrusion below the third button of his shirt. His head was round, shaven, gleamingly ochre. He wore *chinelas* with green felt over the toes. He wore trousers of full length and not rolled above the knees as the fishermen wear them. And these trousers were white drill. Not very new by any means, but neither were they the coarse blue denim that the ordinary folk wore. His white undershirt with its half sleeves was fully visible through his black *barong tagalog* (lacey, transparent shirt).

Though he was born and bred in a village of fishing folk, his face was not the deep-brown that comes from exposure to the sun. It was an oleaginous cream shade which the slightest excitement suffused with pink high up around the eyes. He had never taken to the crude hardships of the sea. He did relish the fare that the sea could provide. But to swing a paddle, to step about a cockleshell of a *banca,* barefooted, tending nets and lines the chill night through, this was something that did not attract him in the least. His mother had him named *Deo Gracias.* The natives promptly shortened it to Gracing. With such a liturgical name, one could not wonder that the Church drew him. As fiscal, he had many duties to which he officiously added more.

The day's work was ended. He took his *kalugong*, a conical-shaped squash helmet, and padded out of the convento. There was a light burning in the church. He had forgotten those candles. He waddled over to the church. Automatically his pudgy finger found the huge shell filled with holy water. There were no windows in the walls, just embrasures; and bats were swooping eerily about. The Padre was kneeling at the altar rail, gazing at the crucifix. With a total lack of tact Gracing approached him and broke in on his prayer.

"The Santo Cristo Milagroso," he whispered, pointing to the crucifix. "You can see better up there." He took the priest's arm and led him up a narrow staircase behind the altar. They came out on a tiny platform in front of the crucifix. Gracing knelt and kissed the foot; the priest followed suit. They left the church. Father Templeton was lonesome and asked to accompany Gracing to his hut. They took the path on the beach.

"That Santo Cristo Milagroso, Padre," stated Gracing, "it is five meters high and two meters wide."

"Indeed?" He was glad to hear the sound of a voice.

"It is maybe three hundred years ago that the cross comes," Gracing declared. "This is all written in the old books in the convento. The day is the one when Santa Helena finds the cross. Our people are then not good people. They are *banditos*, pirates of the sea. They are as brave as the Moros of Mindanao. They come back this day from an expedition. It is May third, huh? And they find here a big box floating on the shore. It is over there," he gestured far up the bay. "It is halfway between Santa Cruz and that barrio of Lugo. They drag the box up on the shore. It is smeared all over with rosin. The mysterious box is opened and inside is a big black crucifix and a small statue of the Virgin Maria. Many people came from Lugo. They shout: 'Milagro! Milagro! (miracle).' There is not even one drop of water on the images. The rosin kept it out. The people from Lugo take hold of the crucifix to carry to their church. Our people grabbed the statue of the Virgin Maria. They cannot move it. Then they changed places. The people of Lugo took the statue and our people took hold of the cross. And it was easy to carry them! So the cross came to us and we are now called Santa Cruz."

They walked in silence for a while, the tide lapping gently on the sands. Gracing's *chinelas* shuffled loosely. The Padre made no comment as the man continued his narrative. "Some Padres came from Manila to study the cross. They say maybe the box floated here from Japan. There is persecution in Japan and the Catholics put the Santo Cristo in the water. There is a current that goes southwest and brings it here." There was a trace of incredulity in his last sentence.

"You don't hold with that, though?" questioned the priest.

"The Santo Cristo is a miracle," stated Gracing sturdily. At once he launched into an account of the wonders that had been wrought by the cross: fishbones removed from throats, wonderful catches of fish, cures of fever. Abreast of the village he halted his narrative and with a *"Muy buenas noches,* Padre," he took leave of the priest.

For a while Father Templeton stood silently beneath one of the tall palms. Splashes of mellow light from cocoanut oil lamps appeared in the surrounding darkness. The pungent smell of burning cocoanut husks met his nostrils. Supper, home, light. People, his people, healthy, happy, at home. He, outside, alone, in doubt, fear still on him. No one to whom he could turn. His fingers slid into his cassock pocket and encountered the crucifix on his rosary. Gracing's story. He mused about it. A dog yapped threateningly.

He moved back to the beach and turned homeward. The fresh breeze of the sea was soft on his cheek. The plushy sand of the beach was like a carpet beneath his feet. It was different here. The sky was reeling with stars. Immensities above and about him. His fear and dissatisfaction seemed such puny things here. Peace came upon him. The sea snuffled on the sand, a soft yet uneasy sound like the murmur of a dreaming child. "Curious," he mused, "the sea never sleeps. Somehow it is like the mind of man, ever restless, ever in motion, even when it seems tranquil and undisturbed. The surface is calm enough and is apparently quiet; but beneath the seeming tranquility there is tremendous movement. It is an elemental thing like the light and the darkness, like the sun and the stars. It is a cosmic thing symbolic in its slumbering restlessness of the history of man and his ceaseless questing and striving."

He gazed out over the water. His dread, his desire to be rid of men, rose up in him with sudden poignancy. Abruptly he turned his back on the sea. It had brought to mind things he wanted to forget. He stalked hastily back toward the convento.

# Chapter IV

A PIG was luxuriously rubbing its hind quarters on a log. In the distance a long white cloud was climbing the slope of the mountain. A pair of men waded in to the shore. Across their shoulders was a pole. The basket suspended from the pole showed a quantity of large, limp fishtails hanging over its edge.

From his haven of shade beneath the buri palm Lacay Luis watched the fishermen. A little later, he shuffled to their hut. In a most casual way he called out a greeting. The response was immediate, "Apo! Lacay Luis?" Yes; it was Lacay Luis. Just a little visit. Oh, they had had a good catch? *Buena suerte! Dac-dacquel!* (How big!) And one a sailfish! Caray! They were good to eat. He chatted with the men and then dozed off quietly in a corner.

When lunchtime arrived he managed to be among those present. No one would ever have thought of refusing him a meal. The simple folk understood him. His presence meant that a meal was expected. With the hospitality traditional among the Filipinos they would never think of speaking roughly to the old man, much less of sending him away. He was welcome. "Will you eat with us, Lacay Luis?" the fisherman's wife asked. The old man looked up, slowly let the lids close down over his eyes in affirmation, and then declared: "An empty sack cannot stand."

Delighted, the woman of the household went laughingly about the meal's preparations. Lacay Luis had earned his meal. Tomorrow when she met the other housewives at the river to do their washing, she would hand on to them Lacay Luis' latest saying. There would be much bantering and laughter about it.

The people were kind to him, but Lacay Luis did not put a strain upon their generous nature. Shrewdly enough the problem of his food supply was distributed equally among them. He did not camp on anyone's threshold. His visits were spread among them and so his welcome never wore out. The men liked him. His fund of sea knowledge was phenomenal. Santa Cruz was the only village he knew.

His whole world was fish, the sea, its salty lessons, and the wisdom gathered from a life among his own kind. His was a ruminative sort of mind. Like the sea, steadily and slowly heaving, then quietly lapping over the pebbles on the beach. His mind would pick up a thought or a fact; like a pebble turned by the waves, he would play with it, study it, look at it from different angles, form his own ideas on it — and never forget them. He was an authority on tides. On the type of fish likely to be running, the most promising spot to let down the nets, on problems of fish corrals and weather, his opinion was invariably sought. He dearly loved to give it, too.

The sea was in the fiber of the old man's soul. The contest between them was not yet over. He could tell others how to meet the sea and wrest from it its treasures. The knowledge was his. His words were few. If he could frame them into a Delphic line he was the happier for it. Invariably his judgment was right. It was a knowledge founded on an infinity of small things — the breeze, the behavior of sea fowl and the small creatures of the bay, the tide, the time, and a general feeling that came to him from the wide sea. How does the bird learn to build its nest? How does the spider learn to weave the intricate pattern of its web? Instinct? There was much of that in Lacay Luis or perhaps what psychologists ticket with the phrase "intuition of experts."

His stomach well filled, the old man dozed beneath the buri palm. When he awoke from his doze it was late afternoon. A white-gowned figure was walking slowly along the water's edge. The old man's eyes followed the figure. Father Templeton looking up, raised his hand to his helmet. "Apo!" called out Lacay Luis in greeting. "Apo!" responded Father Templeton and made his way to the old man's side. They smiled at each other. The priest sat down and removed his helmet. Silence ensued. Mutely they gazed out over the bay. The beach stretched away from them, the ebbtide lipping its murmurous recessional. To the priest the sea was big with God's presence. His soul grew quiet, attuned for things of the spirit.

"Apo!"

"Yes?" replied the priest.

"The sea. It goes out on feet of silk. It comes in, like a fool, stamping. Why?"

"It has moods, Lacay Luis," answered the priest vaguely.

Ignoring the priest's attempt at a solution, the old man answered his own question. "The sea does not like to go away from us. It is sad. Parting is hard. The steps of the sea are like at the funeral, slow and soft. But the sea is glad to come back to us. It rushes in. The noise of its coming is great."

"So that is the meaning of the tempo of the tides?" prompted the priest.

The old man's eyelids dropped affirmatively. There would be no elaboration. He had told his thought. There would be no further discussion of it.

After another long silence, he turned to the priest.

"Yes?" inquired Father Templeton.

The gaunt brown hand of the old man gestured to the moist strip of sand above the edge of the retreating waters. Thousands of little shell-encased creatures were scurrying about. "Sea urchins," he said.

Father Templeton watched them. They stumbled and jolted about awkwardly. "It is a load they carry," ventured the priest. "They bear their own homes upon their backs."

A ghost of a smile fled across the old man's bewrinkled countenance. The priest's reply had been apropos. It gave his thought a jumping-off place.

"The little ones there are like us, Padre," nodded the sage. "They fight the sea. Very small, the urchins on the beach. Very big, the sea. A fisherman is small but he fights the sea."

"But those poor little bedouins of the beach are carrying a load the fisherman doesn't have," objected the priest. "They have to carry their house along when they march against the sea."

"Yes," assented Lacay Luis gravely. "That is their burden — against the sea. Their blessing, too — they can crawl into it and let the sea carry them. The fisherman has a burden, too — wife, children, food. It is not all evil — it keeps him from getting lazy."

"Is laziness so bad?" asked the priest.

The old man's eyes fixed whimsically on the priest's face for a moment. "The Padre teaches that 'in the sweat of thy brow thou shalt eat thy bread.' Last Sunday you said so. Health is happiness. When the sickness is on us we are sad. Work brings health."

Father Templeton sat back. His first estimate of this old man was undergoing a speedy revision. There flared across his mind a sudden thought. Should he entrust to this wise old man the problem that was besetting him? Would he find a remedy for this discouragement, this dread, in that pharmacopoeia of salty wisdom? But then the thought of exposing his cowardice to the people made him go cold all over. Once this old man knew it, it would be village gossip. Suddenly he was aware that the silence between them had been overlong. Turning to Lacay Luis, he surprised a look of curious intentness in the old man's eyes, as though he had been studying, weighing him unawares. He shook it off.

"You do not speak much, Lacay," he protested.

"The wise man speaks with silence," came the simple reply.

The priest rose. "It is getting late. I must go now."

"Adios, Apo."

"Adios, Lacay."

The priest strode down the beach. Lacay Luis' gaze followed the slim retreating figure. There was a curious expression on the old man's face, as though he had asked for something and it had not been given him.

# Chapter V

TOTOY'S mind was absorbed with a problem for which
he had no solution: the Padre ate little, talked less, just
seemed desirous of being alone, and every afternoon since
their coral-gathering expedition took a solitary walk on
the beach. On this afternoon Totoy's curiosity could not
be held in check; quietly he slipped out of the house and
set off after the Padre.

The priest's course led past the village. He moved
slowly on the loose sands of the beach. If any curious eyes
followed him from the village and its screen of palms, he
had no thought for them. Alongside of a ragged jumble
of basaltic rocks above the water's edge, he halted; his
eyes sought the horizon. The day seemed dead with the
heat, and even the glaring light was inert.

As a sail is set to catch the breeze, so was his soul
awaiting some message, some guidance, some word of inspiration. O Lord of the vast seas, was there to be no
answer to his waiting desire? Day after day in the quiet
of this lonely spot he had battled with his fears. And each
day had passed with no ray of hope to light his discouraged soul. His head dropped dejectedly. He compared
himself to one of the sea urchins, a poor impotent mite,
scrambling over life's floor and carrying the shell of his
limitations on his back. A prayer rose to his lips:

"I went into this for You, Lord. I was rash, presumptuous, unaware of how weak I really am. But I did take up this life for You . . . and You can read a man's heart in all its lack of development. Sweep over me with Your supporting strength. Lighten this burden of fear. Let Your inspiring beauty, the heartening peace of Your presence burst over me. Let it not all be Calvary. Grant me at least one moment's glimpse of Thabor."

He turned and walked back from the water's edge, to a cluster of palm trees that grew beyond the rocks.

He could not overcome this fear that choked him, this dread that made him unfit for the ordinary things of life, much less for the heroic.

In every priest, he realized now, there had to be something of the hero. In a missioner, more so. And he — he had not the courage of an ordinary fisherman. His eyes roved out over the bay. The seas were crashing in foam on Magdalen Reef. How well the natives had named it. Patiently the reef took the scourgings of the waves on its back; a mountain on its knees. Absorbed, he watched the waves hiss over the penitent reef. They seemed to swish through the air like whips of liquid glass.

There was a curious comfort in watching the seas lash the reef. Whips of remorse kept stinging him too, but gradually a calmness came to him. The thought arose in him that all things pass: the sharpest trials, the deepest remorse. One but needed the strength to bear the pain of one's own mistakes, the humility to acknowledge them, the patience to face one's errors and weaknesses. Patience — that was life's great lesson. All locks yielded to that key.

A cloud hung above the broad expanse of the sea. Slowly it moved high above him until it came to rest in the arms of a palm tree. Dreamily, enviously, he gazed at the serenity above him. The feeling of calm deepened within him. Fretfulness, tiredness fell from him. What healing in the sea! One had but to open the doors of one's soul and admit its lessons of light and healing.

Peacefully content he lay back and watched other clouds rise from the tundras of the sea. How lovely they were. Wind flowers, marking the sky, as hoar frost writes its message on a windowpane. He wondered why, in this tropical heat, he should be thinking of hoar frost. And then he began to think of snow and ice and the white blanket that clothes the fields in wintertime outside the seminary at home.

A loud cry shattered his reverie. He sat up. Helter-skelter down the beach a small figure came flying. Suddenly it flung forward sprawling on the sand. Springing to his feet the priest raced foward. The prone figure looked familiar. It was Totoy. The priest dropped to his knees beside him.

"Totoy!" he exclaimed.

The boy lifted an intent face. "He hab got away, Faddaire," he said disappointedly.

"What got away? What happened?"

"The crab." His breath came out jerkily with the exclamation, "I will make him come out." He scooped up the dry, loose sand in his young eager hands and poured it into the aperture whither the crab had escaped. The aperture was almost filled when its small inhabitant came struggling through the choking sand for air. Totoy pounced on it. "You can eat this one if you like, Faddaire."

"Like that? Uncooked?" ejaculated the priest.

"Eben," assented the boy. He nipped off the small

claws and demonstrated. The priest took a tentative nibble. It was too wild and raw for his taste, but Totoy seemed to regard it as a delicacy. His crab hunt was but begun. The Padre was enlisted.

The priest's job was to walk along the upper sands of the beach and startle the crabs. Totoy patrolled the water's edge. As Father Templeton kicked up the crabs they dashed frantically in erratic zigzags for the sea. The priest's warning cry would send Totoy darting forward to intercept the escaping prize. Very few got by the alert youngster. Several he caught by falling flat at the water's edge and flattening the victim with his outstretched arm. Some nimble customers would scurry back and disappear in a hole. On these they repeated the smoking-out process, using the dry sand as their weapon.

Soon the spirit of the hunt took possession of the priest. Before he was aware of it he was shouting, running, even diving forward flat in the sand to catch an escaping fugitive. He was lying thus, his hand clasped tightly over a hole, calling to Totoy to come quick, when a quiet voice from nowhere sounded in his ear: "They are very fast" the voice said. Startled, the priest rolled to one side and looked up. Lacay Luis' corrugated face grinned down at him. Blushing furiously, the priest jumped to his feet and started knocking the sand from his soutane and rearranging his attire. "Uh — we were catching crabs," he explained shamefacedly.

"It is much fun," replied the old man understandingly. "I am too old now," he added regretfully. "Not even could I catch a turtle."

Father Templeton's sense of dignity asserted itself. Evidently the old man thought nothing less of him for his

unusual behaviour. Totoy looked slyly up at the priest.
His attitude seemed to say: "We had a good time but now
we must stop. The Lacay cannot run."

The three walked slowly along the beach, Lacay Luis
talking. Father Templeton only half heard him. He was
thinking of the cheery half-hour Totoy had brought him.
What a marvellous faculty this was of boyhood: to evolve
joys from any set of conditions. He needed that faculty.
He looked at Totoy. The boy's whole soul was in his eyes
and ears as he devoured the words of Lacay Luis. Evidently future events did not bother him; they belonged
on the farther side of the horizon, and he would not need
to meet them until they came to his shore. It was part of
the philosophy of the sea. Let down the nets now, the fish
are running. Tomorrow — well, the fish may not be running. True. But tomorrow there may be no need of either
nets or fish.

The old man's voice broke in on his thoughts. "Manolo
is going to his fish corral, Padre. If you like to see he will
take you."

He looked at the *banca*, with the two men in it. He
greeted Ramon and wondered at the contrast between the
young man and the older man whom Lacay Luis had
referred to as Manolo. Where Ramon was of a light complexion, this Manolo was as dark as polished mahogany.
Father Templeton knew him slightly as the *capitán* of
the village, but had not previously studied him at close
quarters. He looked at him now and was impressed by
his strength. He was short and stocky, with broad shoulders
and thick heavily muscled arms and legs. He wore a
floppy straw hat and dungarees which had been rolled up
above his knees. His feet were bare, and the big toe of

each foot was splayed out. He had a slight frown on his
face as part of his habitual expression. He was known for
his ability to hold his tongue. Quietness and dignity enveloped him. The priest watched his plodding movements
as he silently prepared to take them into the *banca*.

The corral indicated by Lacay Luis stood out in the
water a little distance from the shore. To the priest it appeared to be little more than a circular fence of bamboo
poles protruding to a height of about three feet above the
surface of the sea, and anchored by a cluster of poles on
the seaward side, poles that reached up some six feet high
into the air. As the paddles flashed Ramon explained to
Father Templeton how the corral was constructed and
what purpose it was intended to serve.

The corral is really a trap to catch small fish and its
plan is very simple. A spot is chosen where the water is
not more than eight to ten feet deep. Bamboo poles are
driven into the sandy bottom to form a circle whose cir-
cumference is two hundred feet. Between the poles huge
squares of rattan latticework are lashed, forming a cy-
lindrical structure reaching to the sea bottom. In the seg-
ment of the circle nearest the shore line they leave an
aperture thirty feet wide. This is the mouth or entrance
of the corral.

At the opposite side of the structure, that nearest the
open sea, there is an exit door the breadth of which is
about five feet. Only it is not really a door. It is rather a
valve, admitting the fish but preventing them from turning and coming back. This valve leads into a boxlike
structure behind the original circle of bamboo poles. It is
narrow for the swarming fish and they swim to the bottom
seeking an escape. They find one. Another valvelike exit

admits them to the trap proper. This is a four by eight-
foot box, the framework of which is of hardwood and the
sides of rattan latticework.

"The box stays on the bottom," said Ramon, conclud-
ing his explanation, "because we have some rocks on top
of it."

"I don't suppose you catch any big fish in this kind of
trap," ventured Father Templeton.

"No," replied the youth, "the small ones, coral fish,
sardines, small bonito. We pull the box up when it is
full. You will eat some of them for supper."

"Will you have enough left over to sell?" asked the
priest.

"Oh, yes," said Ramon confidently.

When they came abreast of the corral, Ramon lashed
the *banca* to the top of one of the bamboo poles. Cautiously, the priest disembarked. The footing was not of
the best. Just a bamboo pole. Ramon stood at his side and
eagerly explained what was to be done.

"You see, Padre, the school of fish enter by that big
opening on the landward side. They are guided seaward
by the encircling arms of the corral. That leads them to
this V-shaped exit. They squeeze through and find they
cannot get back. The walls of the small square hem them
in. They become excited. They swim to the bottom to
find an opening, a place to escape. They find one. It leads
into that box down there. They get in the box but they
cannot get out. Now we will pull up the box and you will
see all the foolish fish we have in it."

Manolo handed Ramon a rope. He dove and after some
time reappeared. He had attached the rope to the box.
Mightily Manolo and Ramon heaved at the rope. A large

box floated sluggishly to the top. Simultaneously a per-
plexed look spread over Ramon's countenance. "Caray!"
he ejaculated. "There is only two." Father Templeton
could not help smiling. The fish did not look foolish,
they were two lovely tinted coral fish, but Ramon certainly did. They removed the catch and lowered the box.

"I can't understand," complained Ramon aloud. Manolo had left his side and was barefooting his way carefully
around the top of the corral. Father Templeton saw him
suddenly freeze to an attitude of attention and his loud
"Mmmm!" came clearly to the priest's ears. Manolo's
finger pointed stiffly to a spot inside the water of the
corral. Father Templeton looked at the spot indicated. A
huge grey shape lazed there. Menace was in the absolute
immobility of its long-muscled body. Danger emanated
from the blunt hammerlike outline of its head.

"*Ai Yai!*" rasped Ramon hoarsely. "*Tiguron*" (shark)!
Quietly he reached behind him and lifted a heavy spear
from the *banca*. Manolo, swiftly halting him, picked up a
paddle. With a sudden motion he beat the paddle down
flat upon the water. A grey streak flashed through the
entrance of the corral. Openmouthed, the priest turned
to Manolo. His knees felt weak. The frail bamboo felt ter-
rifyingly inadequate, and of a sudden the near-by shore
appeared vastly remote. Manolo was explaining to Ramon.
"You spear the shark. It wrecks the corral. Expensib.
Shark always run away from noise."

Ramon listened and Father Templeton wondered.
"Do they always run from the noise? Suppose he had run
toward it?"

Lacay Luis and Totoy were awaiting them on the shore.
"*Tiguron?*" guessed the old man shrewdly.

"Yes," said Manolo, "We will fish for him tonight."

"You like to come, Padre?" invited Ramon. "It is interesting."

Father Templeton felt as though his heart had ceased to beat. He had not the least desire to meet a shark at any hour of the day, much less on a dark night. How could it be interesting? Suddenly he was aware that Lacay Luis was gazing at him curiously and that the others had fallen silent. He looked at them in a bewildered, half-frightened sort of way.

"Manolo says it is good luck when the Padre is along," coaxed Ramon. They sensed his reluctance. They must not think him afraid. He found sudden speech.

"Sure — sure, I will go," he hastily assented.

That curious expression passed again over Lacay Luis' features. Whether it was a rheumatic pain or deep satisfaction, only the old man himself could tell. Manolo handed Totoy one of the fish.

"Oh, no," objected Father Templeton, "you only caught two. We couldn't take it."

Manolo merely smiled. The matter was closed.

Back in the convento Totoy explained to the priest that he could give Manolo some canned goods in return but that he must not refuse a gift.

"Very well," said the priest. "Here is a box of canned things from Manila. What will we send to him, 'Toy?"

"This one, Faddaire," said the boy promptly.

"But that is sardines," protested the priest. "He can get them fresh here."

"Eben, Faddaire."

Father Templeton shrugged his shoulders. "All right. Take them over to him."

From the veranda he watched the boy go trudging down the beach, the can of sardines held in one hand. They had outlandish ways, this people, but Totoy could be depended on to keep him on the right side of the traffic.

Dusk was falling over the sea. On the glassy water the tops of the fish corral stood up like a circle of white teeth. The thought of the forthcoming expedition made the priest uneasy. "Go among the people." Look what it had dragged him into now! A shark-hunting expedition. What was the sense of it all? Suppose something should miscarry? That murderous shark. He felt a vague sort of emptiness in the pit of his stomach. He sat down. And then a surge of anger at his weakness took hold of him. Was he to go through this at every turn? Couldn't he face any event without that queasy feeling laying hold of him? Why had he gone out to the corral anyhow? That innocent circle of bamboo stems out there in the water was the cause of this. His mind reverted to the conversation with Ramon. Well, he had learned all about a fish corral. It was no longer a maze to him. It had design. There was thought and skill in it. Manolo's pride and care for it was understandable now. It was man's cunning pitted against the natural art of the fish. It was efficient. It earned a living. It was done with the materials at hand. And there was not a single nail in it.

A feeling of pride came over him. He was glad to know all this about the corral. Probably few white men, passing tourists, did know. They just gazed at these things and if they asked, were told they were fish corrals. He knew just how they operated and the ingenuity of the men who constructed them. A curious elation succeeded his vague fears. Manolo — the thought of him gave him confidence. And Manolo thought the Padre was good luck. He went indoors and dug out a valise. Inside he found what he had sought. Coarse, khaki trousers and an old white soft-collared shirt.

# Chapter VI

IT WAS a moonless night. The *banca* slid into the dark water. Paddle in hand, Manolo sat in the stern, Father Templeton in the center, Ramon in the prow. A short stout pole behind Manolo supported a petromax lamp. The two fishermen let drive with their paddles and the *banca* headed out into the waste of waters. Except for the dip of the paddles and the slap of the outriggers as they hit the water and the seething hiss as they slid through the sea, there was no sound. Slap of the wavelet, hiss of the outrigger, a grunted exhalation from the men at the paddles. What a piece of stupidity the whole undertaking was. An infinity of sea all about them, and they were going out into that vastness to hunt and to kill a marauding shark! What would be the chance of meeting with the shark? If they did, what would be their hopes of killing it? His eyes took stock of the equipment in the *banca*. Hooks and lines; a fish spear; a heavy sort of harpoon; a double-barrelled shotgun and a host of other things. The shotgun belonged to Ramon and was loaded with an unusual charge, specially prepared by Ramon. The pellets had been extracted and a large iron ball waxed into position in the shell case. *"Es muy formidable,"* vouchsafed Ramon and Father Templeton had readily believed him, even while he wondered at the boy's clear Spanish.

After an hour of steady paddling Manolo dropped a floating anchor over the side. It was contrived of a weight and a large square of canvas. They drifted quite a distance from this, the *banca's* nose holding steadily into the slight breeze. When finally they came to rest, Manolo drew a bulky parcel from beneath his seat. This was shark bait. He set the line. The wind was in the priest's favor. A glimpse of the carrion was enough. He concentrated his attention on Ramon setting lines for barracuda.

The petromax lamp was lit and cast a brilliant square of radiance as far as the *banca's* outriggers. With triple-pronged hooks, the trio set about snaring squids. The hooks were let down a few feet beneath the water's surface. Intently they gazed over the edge of the boat. A filmy white blob floated over the hook. A swift upward jerk of the line and the squid was snared. At least that is what Manolo did. Adroitly he kept twitching up his victims and dropping them into a can.

Father Templeton, on the other hand, missed five out of every six. Perhaps his thoughts were in some measure the cause of his clumsiness. He could not help but observe what the sea can do to values. Here he was, a person who had had years of study in the classics, sciences, philosophy and theology. Manolo had never read anything except a catechism. Yet the Filipino was the guide, the leader, the guard. The priest felt like a small boy taken out for an excursion by his father. Before making any move he had to ask Manolo if it was the proper thing. In fact, most of the time he was asking questions. And for each of them Manolo had an answer.

Far off in the darkness Father Templeton espied a speck of light. It was another *banca* fishing. Soon other lights winked into existence. Manolo told him what type of fish the newcomers would be after. "Look," he directed. The priest gazed at the tiny speck of light indicated. It was blinking steadily, slowly. "They have found big schools of fish. That is the signal for the others," elucidated Manolo. Soon the other lights began to move slowly toward the signal light. Manolo assured the priest that the occupant of every *banca* was paddling for dear life to get to the scene. The great distance made their progress seem slow.

They fell silent. Lightly the boat rested on the water. High overhead the stars gleamed white and serene. And then with no thought of a warning fear took hold of the priest. The sea can be terrifying by night. Its depths run with swift death. Suppose they tangled with the shark? This peanut shell of a *banca*. Father Templeton's misgivings increased. He was decidedly glad of the light from the lamp. A turn of the head gave him a glimpse of Manolo. Somehow the stocky Filipino brought a measure of confidence to him. There was no fear in that hardy little brown body. This was routine. Imagination was a tool that served him for fashioning corrals and other fish-snaring devices. Outside of that it had no place. Absorption in the task at hand cast out any qualms of fear. Manolo would not be ignorant of the fact that danger was all about them. But the priest had the feeling that every danger had been already met and conquered by this self-reliant little figure. He had a growing conviction that, no matter what betided, Manolo would know what to do, and in his wordless way, would do it swiftly, efficiently.

But in himself the priest knew that imagination was the anvil whereon the first form of fear was shaped. It grew into something more definite with each beat of his heart. His fear became large and unwieldly. Why this should be he did not know — but gradually, as had happened before, he felt it beyond his control. Each new effort to conquer it, to use it to his own good, only seemed to show more clearly the weakness of his heart.

The night wore on. Ramon had no luck with his barracuda lines. The priest began to be sleepy. He was grown weary and cramped from his backless perch. His eyelids drooped. Like a knife, a tense, hard-breathed curse tore through his fogged consciousness. The *banca* quivered. He jerked his head erect. Manolo had galvanized into a tight-jawed dynamo of action. Muscles taut beneath their smooth brown skin, he braced against the thick line. The shark had struck.

Ramon, crouched in the bow, speedily whipped in his lines and cleared things away. The boy seized the shotgun and fixed his eyes on Manolo. Sweat glistened on Manolo's face; his teeth gritted sharply as he played the shark.

Father Templeton slipped to his knees in the bottom of the boat and clamped his hands to the thwarts in a vicelike grip, as he saw a gleaming black shape heave out of the water at the edge of the outrigger. Simultaneously, a nightmare of sudden sounds and sweeping death enveloped him. The shark swung precipitately toward the boat. The line slacked. Frenziedly Manolo reached over to take it in. There was a cracking noise as the shark's body grazed the outrigger. The *banca* gave a violent pitch and Manolo was jolted into the sea. Like a dart, Ramon dropped his gun, leaped over the prostrate priest and seized the line. Manolo's dripping arm came over the side of the *banca*. Frozen with fear, Father Templeton stared helplessly at him; stupidly he noted the water run off the smooth brown skin. Manolo heaved himself over the thwart, his gleaming face pushed close to the priest's. The man's mouth was open, and the salty water moistened the priest's cheek. The fisherman's exhalation of relief fanned his face. Suddenly it contorted and a shriek of pain rang out. The priest's arms closed in a convulsive grasp about Manolo's body, as the shark swept alongside the boat. Perilously the tiny craft lifted, teetered, righted itself. A voice cut through the priest's consciousness. "Pull him in! Pull him in! Quick!" His hands moved. Like an automaton he obeyed. Blood was suddenly all over him. A sick feeling engulfed him. Again the voice, screaming now "*Dios mio!* Padre! The gun, the gun — shoot, shoot!" There it was. That gleaming black shape again, off the edge of the outrigger. A roar of sound rocked the night. Through the priest's shoulder came a sharp stab of pain.

Stupidly he gazed at Ramon. There was a grim satisfaction stealing over the youth's sweat-dripping face. The priest's eyes followed Ramon's intent look. It ran to a spot where the line disappeared in a widening smear of dirty red brown. Ramon held up his open palm. The line barely moved across it. "*Matay-na!* (dead)" he exulted. Then as swiftly he dropped it and bent over Manolo. "*Sus Maria 'Sep!*" came his hoarse whisper. "The leg, Padre, look!"

Fearfully he forced his eyes to look. Relief flooded through him. The leg was there. They straightened the uncomplaining Manolo out. Blood was pumping from a horrible set of gashes in the calf of the leg. Hurriedly the priest took off his shirt and tore it in strips. "It is very lucky. He did not bite the leg off," said Ramon as the priest applied a tourniquet.

" 'Mon, we must get home quick. Get help from the other boats," ordered the priest.

"Some have heard the gun. They will come quick now if I signal," said Ramon.

"Hurry, then, hurry."

Ramon did things with the lamp. Manolo's eyes were closed. Ramon spoke to him: "Is it painful, Manolo?" Manolo opened his eyes. His face had a curious greenish hue in the light of the lamp. "It is painful," he agreed and closed his eyes.

"Lie very still, Manolo," ordered the priest. "The bleeding will stop."

"Yes, Padre," assented the prone figure.

A long pause followed. The priest and Ramon watched the lights of the boats draw closer.

"It was very much noise, eh, Padre?" said Ramon. Father Templeton nodded dully.

"That is because you shoot both barrels at once," grinned the youth.

The priest looked up, startled and amazed. "I — I — did I?"

Ramon's grin widened. "I bet you felt it in the shoulder," he declared.

That sharp pain! It was he, he himself, who had fired the gun and killed the shark.

The boats came up, Ramon shouting the story to them as soon as they were in hailing distance. A swift *banca* quickly took the priest and Manolo on board. Others took charge of Ramon, the battered boat, and the dead shark. As their *banca* charged speedily through the waters,

Father Templeton kept Manolo's foot on his lap. At intervals he loosened the tourniquet to allow circulation.

As soon as the boat grounded on the beach, one of the men ran for the District Sanitary Inspector. Father Templeton and the other man carried Manolo to his house. There were sharply indrawn breaths, a gasp of dismay from Marita, Manolo's eldest daughter, and then quick care. Towels, clean water, and a pillow under the leg. The Sanitary Inspector came. He glanced at the leg. "Hmm. Tiguron, eh?" he said, in a matter-of-fact tone of voice. Methodically he put out some instruments and set to work. He had done this before. His hands were sure, deft.

When the stitching was done the priest asked a careful question. "There is no — no danger, doctor?"

The little man looked up. "Danger?" he seemed to be fumbling for the priest's meaning. "Oh, you mean will he die?" He laughed. "Not Manolo. Small but terrible — that's Manolo." He grinned at his patient. "Maybe if the tiguron bit off the two legs — but then, only, maybe."

Day was breaking in great glories of color over the bay when Father Templeton entered the convento. Totoy gave one glance at him, half-naked, blood-spattered, and his face went a curious color. "Faddaire!" he ejaculated. "You are full of bloods!"

"It's not mine. It's Manolo's."

"He is hurt? The tiguron hab killed him?"

Wearily the priest washed, detailing the story. He felt suddenly weak and found his way abruptly to a chair.

"You are hurt too, Faddaire?"

"No, 'Toy," said the priest, managing a smile at 'Toy's solicitous look. "Not hurt at all. I'm just more — " he bit his lip — "more shaken up than anything else."

A sudden reaction swept him. The full realization of his narrow escape was but a small thing. He saw himself again crouched in the bottom of the boat — frozen with fear — not lifting a hand to help Manolo into the boat. . . . His face flushed at the memory of it, and he felt a wave of embarrassment sweep over him. On his clenched hands the knuckles showed white, as he tried to conquer the memory of his cowardice. He could set his will to a task, he knew; but he had learned the bitter lesson that his will was not everything. In his soul, as in every man's, there was a perpetual conflict: flesh against spirit. The higher against the lower, and the lower against the higher. Even his favorite saint, the energetic tentmaker of Tarsus, had known the same bitter struggle within the confines of his own being. "There is another law within my members," he had once written. And Frank Templeton was now beginning to savor the meaning of St. Paul's very human plaint.

Another law within my members! The law of manliness on the one hand, and the other law of cowardice, of weakness, of stark paralysing fear. He resolved to fight that other law of his being, to conquer it, to destroy it. Oh, but how? How? Wishing and willing were mere words out of a dictionary. What was his will to mean when he was again face to face with a challenge to his courage?

He lifted his eyes, suddenly aware of the boy's presence. "I . . . I'll lie down now, 'Toy," he mumbled. The boy stole from the room. The Father wanted to be alone.

# FAITH:

"At thy word I will lower the net . . ."
*(Peter to Christ)*.

# Chapter VII

1

THE morning was pleasant with a light breeze over the sea. The sun had come up, and the sea shone like polished glass. Sturdily the little interisland steamer chugged through the waters.

"Retreat do you any good?" asked Father Conners.

Father Templeton's eyes remained fastened on the sea. "The retreat?" he mused. "Yes; it did me good. I'd be on another steamer otherwise — a bigger one — going in another direction — home." He placed his sun helmet on the deck beside his chair. Nervously he ran his hand through his crisp dark hair. "The — atmosphere was very frigid."

Father Conners drummed his blunt, strong fingers on the sun helmet he held on his lap. He had noticed the cool attitude of the others toward Frank. But what could the boy expect? He had yet to prove himself. "That will wear off," he assured the other heartily.

Father Templeton shook his head. "I don't think it will," was his gloomy response. "And I really don't much care about their estimate of me. But," he added, and a wistful note crept into his voice, "I would like to have the good will, the respect of my own people."

Father Conners looked up quickly. *His own people.* Hmm. Things were looking up. "I think you have made a start in that direction," he replied in a flat conversational tone to keep the elation out of his voice. "I never did tell you how, some months ago, Totoy recounted to me the story of your killing the shark. You were quite a hero in his eyes."

"In his eyes, yes," retorted the other bitterly. "He wasn't there. If I hadn't been scared stiff, Manolo would not have had that mangled leg."

"But you did shoot the gun and saved the lives of the three of you," persisted Father Conners.

"I have told you, Buff," protested Father Templeton a trifle irritably, "I have no recollection of that. I was frozen, unconscious with fear. It was Ramon's will that acted, not mine."

"But you did it," insisted Buff.

"Manolo knows differently. He is a reticent man. Were he to speak out — were he to tell all the facts of that affair — well, I would have left Santa Cruz long ago. I couldn't hold up my head. I made no move to help him in the boat. All that mattered was my safety. My hands held me in the boat. Manolo saw my face. He knows. He read my soul then. He saw, Buff, and saw clearly that I am a coward." He paused. "And it was his desire that I go with them on that trip, he thought the priest brought good luck. It almost cost the unfortunate man his life," he finished bitterly.

A long silence fell between them. Numerous flights of startled flying fish broke from the side of the boat. Idly the two priests watched them flash through the air, silver darts that gleamed in the tropic light and suddenly plummeted back into the water. Half to himself, half aloud, Father Templeton mused: "That's a picture of me. A creature that has kicked its way out of its element — into the glorious heroism of mission life. . . . But it is not my element. . . . I can't sustain myself in it. . . . I wasn't made for it. . . . The sooner I get back to the States, the better for me. . . ."

"Look, Frank," broke in Buff abruptly. "Let's cut out this defeatist business. You have made a start. You grabbed the stick by the wrong handle and instead of encouragement you got an additional jolt. All right. I never intended you to start fighting sharks when I told you to get among the people. I meant something entirely different."

"What did you mean then?"

"Shucks!" protested Buff. "A priest's job is not with harpoons and shotguns. It's with souls. You've got to go among them in their ordinary pursuits. I mean their homes, sickness, fiestas, and the like. They've got a lot to give you in the example of simple courage. And you've got a lot more to give them in the line of sympathy, understanding, and God's help. You haven't done that yet."

The young priest's brow wrinkled. "Why, that is just what I thought I was doing," he protested.

The older man looked at him quizzically for a moment. "Tell me, Frank, just how many people do you personally know in Santa Cruz?"

Frank sat up a bit straighter. "Well, there's Lacay Luis."

"A fine character. But he is past the period where he has problems. He doesn't need your help."

"Gracing and Totoy."

"They work for you," smiled Buff. "You couldn't help knowing them. Unless you were deaf, dumb, and blind."

"Well, Manolo and Ramon."

"You made a trip with them," assented the other. "Who else?" Father Templeton was silent. The enumeration was complete.

"You see what I mean, Frank?"

Father Templeton was buried in thought for a moment. "I guess I do, Buff," he finally said. "There are others I know by name but I haven't really gone among them and so — the year has been practically wasted. But those two episodes took a lot out of me. I felt so disgraced. I wanted to be alone. I prayed enough, God knows. I don't seem to have received any light as to what I was to do and — I just could not risk another failure."

"All right, let's skip that now," said Buff with a sweeping gesture of his hand. "Here's the next item on the program. Concentrate on meeting as many people as possible each day. Talk to them. Find out their troubles. Interest yourself in them. Try to help them."

"That will not be as hard as I thought last year," said Frank.

"Don't fool yourself. It's going to take courage. You may have to make enemies. You will have to do a lot of things that you would sooner leave undone. But the people will appreciate your help. They'll show you that they welcome you. They'll be glad to talk to you."

"At least, I've got something definite to work on, Buff," said the other. His eyes roved out over the sea to a bastion of rocks guarding a strip of shore. "You're the only one that has taken any interest in me, Buff, and — thanks."

"Nonsense, Frank. As an old missioner, I hate waste in all its forms. And there's a whale of a lot of waste in your life, waste of natural abilities, waste of talents, waste of opportunities to do God's work. Pull yourself together, Frank. The job is waiting for you. Fields white for the harvest, you know."

2

Not a soul was at the rickety pier to greet them as they disembarked at Santa Cruz. Silently they strode up the dusty highway. The long road, its dust merging into the stretch of pulverized white coral, was grown familiar to Father Templeton. He had seen it in the dreariness of the rainy season and in the long golden months of the rest of the year. There was always life along it: boys with water tubes, carts, a calesa. He passed people with a half nod or a halting word of greeting.

Buff said nothing. They trudged on in a curious silence, the powdery dust puffing up from their plodding shoes. Frank's eyes lifted. The long straight road merged into the corals — a white ribbon, sentinelled with the lush regal palms. White the road — white, like a bleached bone. A graveyard had dry white walks like this. As far as he was concerned, this walk was always a death walk. Life surged by him but never touched him. He was a spectre.

Suddenly the road became a symbol. This was what Buff had meant. To his village's main street he was a stranger, unknown to the people that trod it. He did not belong. His going or his coming made no mark on the people's calendar, caused no throb of interest. If he was present the bell would ring in the morning and there would be Mass. If he was absent, it would not. This was the total result of a year's residence! The thought bit deep and bitterly. He turned to his silent companion.

"Buff, does anybody come to meet you when you arrive at your station?"

Buff looked at him queerly. "Yes."

"I'll bet it's quite a crowd," ventured Father Templeton.

"Well, yes. There usually is a crowd, Frank. I married half of them and baptized the other half. Guess the only ones who aren't there are the ones I buried. You see, I've been there for years and years."


3


Totoy began removing the dishes from the supper table, while Father Templeton strolled out to the veranda. Buff had told the truth. Totoy's glances, his eager readiness to anticipate his every wish, his evident gladness at his return, were all tinged with a bit of hero worship. Strange, and he such a coward.

The full warm dark of night came down on sea and sky and mountain. One star stood immobile over the bay. A world apart, staring down upon him. A thing of ineffable beauty. His thoughts strayed. What would be the appearance of this globe of ours, viewed from that far-off star? Would it, too, gleam beautiful, serene, silent with loveliness, all its blotches obliterated by the magic of distance? Distance, a difference of viewpoint, how that could change a thing's appearance!

A naked foot thudded softly on the veranda. He turned.

"You do not want the lamp, Faddaire?" The boy held the lamp before him. Its light gilded the brown shoulders, the white of his *camisa,* and brought out the strange eager light in his eyes.

"No, 'Toy," said the priest.

The boy half turned and then faced the priest again. "There . . . there is something else, Faddaire?" he questioned hopefully.

The priest smiled. "No, chico. I like it like this. . . ." His hand gestured toward the dark and the sky beyond the veranda.

Totoy bowed and went away. His brow a trifle puckered, the priest went back to the veranda rail. Buff had been right. 'Toy did think him a hero.

The multitudinous sound of insect life filled his ears. Cicadas, cocoanut beetles, scraping, buzzing, an unending tuneless symphony, rising and falling. It was a prayer . . . rising, impetrating . . . falling, aware of the lowliness of the petitioner. A tiny creature's plea.

The feeling so often repeated came over him. Expectancy. Tropic nights begot that feeling in him. The softness of the evening air, the silent watchfulness of the skies, the solemn attention of the drooping fronds of the palms. Expectation . . . tense expectation. His shoulders lifted in a sigh. He was too sensitive to things of this sort. What was he expecting? Buff had outlined his course for him. He knew what he must do.

# 4

He walked through the quiet house, down the steps and toward the church. The gloom of its grotesque entrance reached out and swallowed him. It was not a frightening dark. It was friendly. After the freshness of the air from the bay the atmosphere of the church was musty. The red lamp of the tabernacle flickered a welcome. He knelt down and looked at the crucifix above the altar. This was the miraculous crucifix of which Gracing had spoken. Its black features, glistening with fragrant balsam, looked alive. The flaring of the light across it made the features seem to move. It was easy to pray here. The words came readily. Petitions, the admission of his own weakness, Buff's advice, his inability to see the use of it, his desire to do it, his loneliness. Entrusted with the saving of others, and not captain of his own spirit. How could he lead them?

And then he remembered that the great Apostle wrote that power is made perfect in infirmity. Certainly he was sunken in infirmity, in weakness, in utter cowardice. Long ago he had given up the task of finding out the reason for his lack of courage. He was a coward, he knew; and what was he going to do about it?

He couldn't think of St. Paul as a coward, and yet the Apostle had found that God's grace was the corrective for weakness such as his. "My grace is sufficient for thee." Was that the answer at last? Was an Apostle's power to be considered in terms of that Apostle's weakness? Evidently that was St. Paul's great thought. An Apostle's power is God's power, working through a weak human instrument. To re-create a soul, to redeem a soul is not man's work at all. It is God's work; and the man is merely the instrument that fits into God's hand.

When this thought came to him, he was seized with a sudden sense of how wrongly he had been attacking his problem. He began to see that, instead of his own weakness, he should be thinking of God's omnipotence. Was there not in the Christian soul a quality of readiness that makes a man fit into God's plans as perfectly as a glove fits a hand? So there was the answer, the finally satisfying answer to all his fears.

He began to pray, asking for the gift of readiness to do God's work as a priest. He did not ask for light to see, or strength to do, or courage to dare. They seemed to him to be secondary to the great thought that, no matter how poor and weak and lowly he was in himself, he was God's ordained instrument. He asked simply that he should think no more of his own infirmities but only of God's strength and power. "Lord, Lord, do with me what Thou wilt."

Absorbed, he lost track of time. His eyes stayed fixed on the pitiful features of the gleaming black crucifix. The features vanished, the thorn-crowned head was no longer visible. He saw, framed between the two nail-pierced hands, a squalid hut and a white-gowned figure slowly picking its way up the bamboo ladder that gave entrance to it. The figure walked up and on into the hut and thence right through the hut and entered into a narrow lane.

As the figure passed along this lane, clouds of fine dust puffed up at each step, *tiendas* lined the street. The white-gowned figure entered one, then another, and another. Sordid, squalid places. The odor was overpowering. A dank fishy smell. The white-gowned figure was not averse to it. For now it was squatting before a huge square of fish. The sun beat down, drying the fish. A native squatted beside him. They laughed. The native handed the white-gowned figure one of the drying fish. He bit off a piece. The natives did likewise. The two laughed. And the laughter grew and swelled, till many people were laughing, and above it all rose the clear joyous laughter of the white-gowned figure. About him squatted chattering, laughing women, their shoulders and arms bare, wooden paddles flashing in the sun, water gleaming as the river brawled by, wooden paddles going thump, thump as they beat the clothes. *Lavenderas* (washwomen) at the stream.

The picture faded, the stream dwindled till it became a jet of water spurting from an iron pipe. A loathsome figure crawled toward the jet of water. Thirst was written all over its agonized features. It fell in the dust. People stood and watched. The white-gowned figure appeared, a cocoa-nut shell in his hand. He bent low and the sprawled figure took the cup. The face was horrible. Bloated, disease-blotched. The awful face grew and enlarged before Father Templeton's eyes. It blackened, contorted, lengthened, and suddenly he found himself looking into the infinitely pitiful face of the crucifix.

The priest dropped his head in his hands. These places and people — he knew them. What did it mean? Slowly, overwhelmingly, like the tide taking possession of the shore, a definite conviction took possession of him. This was what was wanted of him! No; it was not just this.

A curious feeling was upon him, as though he had already lived all these things; what was desired of him was a continuance of it. He rose from his knees. His path lay clear before him. His heart was filled with a quiet strength, an eager resolve.

Strangely enough, there was no questioning of the occurrence's reality. Not the faintest misgiving crossed his mind as to whether he had been the victim of an hallucination. There was no awed or shaken feeling in his soul, as though he had witnessed some phenomenon above the natural. His faith was deep; it accepted such things without soul-searching analysis and queries. But in a corner of his brain one small irritation flicked at his peace. That jet of water. There was no well here. Nor had he ever seen that misshapen creature. He went thoughtfully from the church.

# Chapter VIII

IT WAS an hour after dawn, and the sea was alive with life and color. Dancing, leaping, foaming, the waves came tumbling in. Father Templeton stopped and breathed deeply. Something stirred in his soul. Lifting his head he strode eagerly forward. At the edge of the shore he stopped. Totoy plunged heedlessly ahead. People were hastening from the village. The priest stood still. Those lonesome months seemed a thing of the dim past: those dreary weeks when he had walked the sands and taken his fill of the mountains. They had indeed been lonesome hours for him. A group of children chasing sand crabs, a skulking dog venturing forth from the village grove to the sand in quest of food had been for him an event. He had certainly lived a life apart.

It was all changed now. The fishing fleet was in. About him boiled life and activity. Several *bancas* were already anchored in shallow water. Others were still coming in with their single sails set and their outriggers flashing as they lifted clear of the water and caught the sun. Men, women, children streamed down to the water's edge and waded out to the *bancas*. The women pulled up their wrap-around skirts, gathered them in one hand high above the knees and clasping a wicker tray in the other hand splashed eagerly out into the water. A trifle self-

consciously the priest walked down to the water's edge.
A *banca* dropped its sail. At once a group of waders hailed
it with cries, "Many?"

"Yes; many."

"What?"

"Tanguigui!" and the announcer's voice drew out the
last syllable long and loud. At once a group of the curious
were at the gunwales peering into the bottom of the
boat.

"*Ala-a-!*" shouted another exultant arrival. "*Tuyo!
Adu!* (sardines! many)." Like a swarm another group
clustered about the boat. They reached in and fingered
the glistening, firm bodies of the fish. Eager hands trans-
ferred them to the big shallow trays of woven fibre. Then
back to the shore splashed the women, one hand holding
up the gathered skirts in the middle, the other at the edge
of the tray balanced gracefully on the head.

Soon the shore became a bickering, thronging market
place. No one paid any attention to Father Templeton.
The mounded trays were counters about which the
natives squatted. Housekeepers, storekeepers, *commer-
ciantes,* who would sell the produce in distant towns, entered into a brisk traffic. "This pampano? — 25 centavos!"
Father Templeton smiled at their absorption, at the
shrewd bargaining, the continuous fingering and hefting
of the fish. No scales seemed to be needed for this free
and easy trading. His attention was drawn to a *banca*
near shore. Across its scimitar-shaped bow was painted in
glaring white letters — *Napoleon*. A small, bronzed familiar figure, naked save for a pair of dungaress rolled high
on his thighs, put a broad hat of woven buri palm upon
his head and busied himself about the mast. He wrapped

the sail about it, stepped over the *banca's* side, shouldered the sail and trudged stolidly through the shallow water toward the shore. It was Manolo.

The youngest son of the Manolo household stood expectantly. The water reached his chubby knees. Manolo paused, took the child's hand, clasped its soft, yielding trustfulness in his own corded, work-roughened palm, and together they walked slowly up onto the dry, white, yielding sand of the shore. For a moment he paused to greet a woman. Father Templeton recognized her as Manolo's wife, Isabela. She was retailing a large pampano. Manolo made no comment. Father Templeton drew closer. A slat of a Chinaman was fingering the produce. Hunkered on his heels, the loose pants of the Oriental were pulled up high. His shirttail was in the sand and the thin yellow face impassive. He lifted the fish "This one?" he inquired.

Isabela, comfortable, buxom, gave it a glance, "Forty-five centavos."

"Too much, too much," protested the Chinaman.

The crafty Oriental paused. Behind the almond-shaped eyes his thoughts were racing. She said forty-five, that means forty-two is the lowest. "Forty centavos," he offered.

"*Aba!*" exclaimed Isabela disgustedly.

The Chinaman picked up two large bonitos. "How much these?" he queried.

"Seventy-five centavos — each," came the swift reply.

He quoted seventy centavos. The haggling waxed warm. A whisper at Father Templeton's side made him aware of Totoy's presence. "Isabela wants forty-two centavos for the pampano and seventy-two centavos for the bonito," he explained.

"That is one peso and eighty-six centavos in all," said the priest. Totoy nodded assent.

The Chinaman drew out a purse. "One peso, eighty-five for the three," he offered.

"*Justo-na!*" (That is satisfactory) snapped Isabela. The money changed hands. A withe of rattan was run through the gills of the fish, and the Chinaman left, well pleased with his purchase. His face showed no sign of satisfaction, but he had paid one centavo less than her bottom price.

Isabela looked up at Manolo. She smiled. "I added five centavos to the bottom price, Maning," she explained.

Manolo's face split in a grin. His wife had anticipated a hard deal. It was good to come home and know the fish would bring what they were worth. He caught sight of Father Templeton. Dropping the child's hand, Manolo swept his hat from his head. "Apo."

"Good morning," rejoined the priest cordially. "*Suerte,* eh?" His quick glance took in the large medal secured about Manolo's neck by a piece of string. Isabela rose hastily, shaking out her skirt.

"Ap-o-o," she greeted, her voice miraculously changed into a low melodious greeting.

"Isabela, the bargain was good," he commended.

She smiled, well pleased. "It is hard to beat the Chino," she said.

Father Templeton fell into step alongside of Manolo. All about them little groups were squatting around trays of fish. Manolo walked a bit wearily, while Totoy kept plying him with questions. His replies were kind but brief. "The pampano? They struck about midnight. No; not many. He was on the edge of that run. The bonito; yes, much better."

They entered the shade of the encircling palms. At the edge of the largest dwelling Manolo dropped his burden. *"Morisqueta* (boiled rice) ready, Father!" sang out a clear soprano voice. In the doorway appeared a slim girl. A simple print dress. Eyes black and gleaming like chico seeds looked full at the priest. "Marita, this is the Padre," said Manolo.

"Good morning, Father," said the girl shyly.

"Good morning, Marita."

"This is the oldest," explained Manolo, motioning Father Templeton and Totoy into the house. Manolo took a coarse towel and returned to the beach. He waded out up to his neck. Bathed, his weariness gone, the salt water still stinging his eyes, he toweled his head vigorously as he tramped back to his dwelling. While he ate heartily of the steaming rice and fish before him, Father Templeton chatted with Marita. She was a lovely slip of a girl, eighteen years old, her complexion a luscious olive, her hair a wealth of thick straight black tresses neatly plaited. There was an indefinable sense of health and neatness about her. With some pride she showed the priest her white dress, blue sash and religious medal. She had formerly been head of the Children of Mary. Was he not going to start them again? Father Templeton, with a smile, promised that meetings would be called this very week. Isabela entered, her *panuelo* (handkerchief) bulging with coins. When she told Manolo the total, a smile of satisfaction lit her face. He rose and accompanied the priest to the door.

"How is the leg now, Manolo?" asked the priest. Manolo's eyes took on a curious, intent stare. There was something of reproach, of coldness in them. For a flashing

moment the priest thought he was looking into the eyes
of his Superior in Minandang on that memorable day a
year ago. Then the expression fled. "It is all right, Apo,"
said Manolo and he stretched the leg forward. Purplish
scars stood out on it lividly.

Totoy was swiftly on his knees fingering the leg, con-
siderably impressed. Manolo grinned.

"You can read it, 'Toy, eh?" he queried. Totoy looked
up shyly. "No. What does it say?"

"*Tiguron*" (shark) laughed Manolo.

"He hab big penpoints," said Totoy, and everyone
laughed at his rejoinder.

Back on the beach Totoy pointed out to the priest a
young lad paddling the *Napoleon* in to shore. "That is
Pablo, Manolo's other boy," he vouchsafed. The *banca*
touched bottom. The youngster carried all its contents,
paddles, lantern, nets up on the shore and then sloshed
buckets of water over the interior of the boat, then hastily
bailed it out. With the aid of some neighbors, the *banca*
was run high up on the sand. "Now he wash the nets,"
said Totoy as the boy took the bundle of dark brown,
dripping lace. He spread them out quickly and ran
through them removing bits of sea-weed, coral, noting the
rents. To dry them he spread them between several palm
trees. The lines were unravelled and dried. Manolo had
drilled all these things into him. It was a lesson for life.
Tackle was their means of livelihood. It cost money. It
would give service only if cared for and kept in condition.

Ramon sauntered up and began to help the boy. The
priest watched him. His carriage, his complexion, more a
copper brown than a Filipino gold bronze. There was
something different about this youth. It had impressed

him on their coral-collecting trip. His features and his
bearing marked him as someone apart.

"Faddaire," confided Totoy, "th-a-a-t Ramon and Manolo hab plan."

"Indeed?"

"They will get some of the cogon lands from Manila."

"What? Get land from Manila?"

"The land is here, Faddaire," said Totoy half-reproach-
fully, "but the government in Manila must gib
permission."

"Oh, I see."

"Then they will burn the cogon and make fish ponds."

"Fish ponds? Aren't there enough fish here in the sea?"

"Oh many, Faddaire. But it is easy to get fish from the
ponds, and to catch them in the ocean at night is berry
hard and dan-ger-ous."

"I understand. Why don't they go ahead?"

"It costs money."

"I suppose. Where will they get it?"

"They will save, Faddaire."

"Oh." Then, after a pause, "It will take a great deal of
time, I suppose?"

"Never mind that, Faddaire. Just be patient."

There it was again. Patience. It would take more than
a few years of skimping and saving to get the required
amount. Manolo would win over that obstacle. He was
sure of it. The simple fisherman was in possession of the
discovery that he himself had made only after long hours
of thought. Patience unlocks all keys. Where had he
learned that?

Father Templeton felt singularly well pleased. He had
found his first attempt delightful. Only one thing irked

him. That quiet glance of Manolo's when he questioned him about his leg. It left a vague disturbance within his mind. Manolo had not forgotten. To that one simple fisherman, his cowardice was known. No word of accusation had ever passed the man's lips. And yet it would have taken but a single word from him to have made of the priest an outcast. A surge of gratitude went over him toward the Filipino, even while he realized that in Manolo's own mind he was not yet fully accepted. He had to prove himself. Well, maybe some day God would provide the opportunity. Meanwhile he had begun to put Buff's advice into practice. And he felt he had put his hand to a good work.

# Chapter IX

## 1

THE rainy season was setting in and it had rained copiously that afternoon. Dull lights, shaded lights began to cut squares of radiance in the blackness that shrouded the street. Far off in the west, the sky was slashed by a long slit of green light. The day was dying. The Angelus bell sent forth its summons. There was the cool, soft sound of water dripping from the palms.

The sound of the drops impinged on the priest's tired brain. It had been a month of ceaseless activity. Four, five, six. Unconsciously he was counting the drops. Seven, eight, nine. His mind roved over the tragedy of it all — ten, eleven, twelve. They had gone like that — thirteen, fourteen, fifteen, sixteen into death, seventeen, eighteen, nineteen. Death was inescapable. But it was hard to see children die, children with life's laughter just beginning to bubble from their lips. Thirty of them. Thirty, within a few days. The thought that those thirty young lives might so easily have been saved added to his sadness.

Going among the villagers daily had brought a curious change in him. Perhaps it wasn't what Buff wanted, but he could not help it. His sympathies were too quick. In this epidemic each death had brought as much grief to him as to the stricken family. He had laboured to save, even when the child's own parents despaired. Success had not crowned his efforts. He felt so impotent before it all and yet there must be something that could be done. He was worn out. 'Toy had only seen him these past weeks at mealtimes. It wasn't just the endless going from house to house. Physical fatigue is swift to mend, but a burden of sorrow lies on the soul like a suffocating weight.

He picked up the book again. "Treatise on Tropical Diseases."

"Apo!" said a quiet voice.

He looked up a trifle startled. "Manolo." He rose quickly to his feet. "Good evening."

The fisherman gestured away the proffered chair. "It is the little one, Apo. Ernesto — sick."

The priest put the book down carefully. "Is it — ?"

"Yes, Apo," said Manolo. "Dysenteria."

Father Templeton quickly took his few medicines and went off with Manolo through the darkness. The rain was pattering down lightly. In an hour it would be a hard drumming downpour that would last through the night.

The two men climbed the ladder of Manolo's house. On a mat on the floor lay the little sufferer. The light of a cocoanut-oil lamp cast its mellow glow about the poor room. Isabela and Marita squatted at the child's side. The priest knelt beside them. There was little he could do. The child was dying. To no avail, he administered the remedies he had. In an hour, the child was dead. Marita and her mother cried brokenly. The priest walked to a corner of the room. Manolo, his face contorted in the room's uneven light, approached him. The priest remem-

bered him wading in to shore after night fishing and recalled that this dead little lad had held his hand, trust-
fully, confidingly, as only a child could. Now it was for-
ever withdrawn. Manolo's corded fingers had not the
strength to hold the child from this despoiler. Death had
broken that handclasp. It must be bitter for Manolo's
quiet love.

"Tomorrow, Padre?"

"Yes, Manolo. At eight o'clock?"

"Yes, Apo." The back of his hand moved awkwardly
over the corner of his eye.

The priest stayed in the stricken home for some hours.
The first spasm of grief past, Isabela made some hot cocoa.
They sipped the liquid and in low tones arranged for the
funeral.

Quietly the priest went from the house. Rain slashed
through the palm fronds. Oblivious of the ooze underfoot, he stepped slowly up the muddied path. Ernesto —
thirty-one. What was to be done? It tore his heart to see
the sorrow of his people. He was ready to take the burden
of all dysentery himself if that would stop it. He had
prayed that just some such thing would happen. But then
God does not work miracles needlessly. This was a thing
that men could combat with proper medical care and pre-
caution. But he had no medical skill and very little
medical knowledge. One thing he had learned. These
dysentery epidemics were periodic. He had talked with
the doctor and they agreed that the rains contaminated
the drinking supply. In his distress his mind was set on
two things. First, he determined to have all the villagers
inoculated as soon as possible; and second, he must
move heaven and earth to ensure a proper water-supply

for the people. Full of these thoughts he sloshed through the rain-noisy dark of the night. It was not going to be an easy thing to interest the proper authorities in Manila, but his own small courage was inflamed at the memory of the restrained sorrow, the mute courage he had just witnessed. The light of the convento beamed up ahead. He was wet through and through. But a fire of indignation burned within him. He was not going to stand idly by and see his people die. He vowed, with God's help, there would be no epidemic next year.

2

It was a procession of supplication. There was no music with it. Prayers in a plaintive key rose and fell, as though the faith of the people were complaining. They believed in God and trusted Him. Why had He allowed this calamity to befall them? Why did He continue to scourge them?

It was late afternoon and a funereal darkness enveloped the landscape. Rain was starting to fall. From his place behind the cross Father Templeton gazed down the line of candles ahead of him. They were passing through the center of the village. It had grown strangely dark, and the main street was like a tunnel. They had buried Ernesto that morning and Manolo had asked in the name of the village for this procession. It had been done before, he explained, whenever a public calamity befell them. The miraculous cross carried through the village would be sure to alleviate the trial. The priest's prayers mingled with his people's as the cortege wound back to the church.

It had been a strain on Father Templeton. All day he had felt ill and feverish. He stole out to the chill coolness of the dark veranda. The rain was falling harder, the wind rising. There was the noise of crashing waves. In the gloom he saw the water rise in long grey combers and with banners of spindrift flying from their summits crash onto the sands.

Life was like that, a sea, a shoreless sea, whipped by relentless and sleepless winds, and the faith of man the only rock that abides. His people's faith . . . how it moved him! What courage he found for his own trial in their method of meeting theirs. It was a lesson read from the heart staring out of their eyes. Suddenly the storm burst over the village. A flame of lightning streaked through the pall of clouds. Thunder shattered the wind-noises of the bay. Full darkness came down on the landscape. He stood there long in the darkness, the roaring of the sea joining its angry bellow to the whistling of the wind. But he paid no heed to the elements. He was thinking about his people and their needs, and he was silently praying that God would give him the strength to be of help to them.

He shivered and caught his breath sharply as a series of spasmodic pains took hold of him. Suddenly he was cold, chilled and sick. His feet stumbled as he entered the house.

"It is a big storm outside, Faddaire," said Totoy.

"There is a big storm inside . . . of me," said the priest, slumping limply into a chair.

Totoy shot a quick glance at the colorless face. "You are sick, Faddaire?" came the solicitous query.

"Very much so."

"It is fever, Faddaire?"

"No; this is our friend . . . dysentery."

He got to his room and tumbled into bed.

Outside the weather became worse. The wind rose and swelled into a typhoon. Its high-pitched key told the story of death and destruction carried in its train. The villagers were busy slinging ropes over the roofs of their huts and pegging them to the ground with long stakes in an effort to save the frail buildings. Palms whipped about madly. Cocoanuts fell with dull abruptness into the welter of water and mud beneath. Rain cascaded down in driving sheets, and the entire bay was lashed and whipped into a nightmare of frenzy.

Oblivious of it all, Totoy laboured at the writing of a note. Manolo must take it to Father Connors as soon as the storm had subsided. A groan from Father Templeton's room spurred him on. "It is the dysenteria," he painstakingly wrote, "and the Father says it is ameebick . . ."

# Chapter X

THE fisherfolk called it Shining Mountain. It rose in a gradual slope from behind the village and its towering peak commanded the broad bay. The day's first gleams of glory gilded it in the morning, and at dusk the sun's last light touched its summit.

At the base of this lordly mountain slope was the hacienda of Don Ernesto de Hierro y Martinez. Father Templeton, peaked and pale after his weeks of illness, stepped from the cart and entered the wide arched gate. He stopped and caught his breath. An immaculate road swept up to a two-storied, latticed, porticoed, balconied edifice. The spaciousness of the white building was typical of the days of Spanish affluence. In the gardens that fronted the building were tastefully arranged tropical plants: fern trees, exotic orchids, poinsettias, palms, and rare shrubs in bewildering profusion. Gracing had told him that Don Ernesto had gathered many plants from the tropic jungles further inland and with rare skill and at no small expense had arranged his gardens and cared for them. Gracing's account had not prepared him for such a fairyland of coolness and color. No wonder the village folk called it "Casa Grande." It was not just big; it was grand, palatial. He walked slowly up the path, his eyes revelling in this vista of growing things and many-coloured loveliness. A middle-aged gentleman, clad in immaculate drill and with a black mourning band about his left arm, met him at the entrance to the house.

The man was of medium height and held himself stiffly erect. His whole demeanour spoke of neatness, trimness, exactness. His dark eyes were set deep, but their depth was corrected by the short sharp nose. The mouth was soft; snowy-white teeth gleamed beneath the clipped grey moustache. The man's expression was gentle. A questioning smile greeted the priest.

"Don Ernesto?" inquired Father Templeton.

"*Si, Padre,*" assented the dapper little figure.

"I am Father Templeton," extending his hand.

"*Servidor de usted,*" replied the other with a courtly bow, as he stooped over the priest's hand.

"I am at a loss for words," said the priest smiling and hesitant. He turned and spread his hands in a happy gesture. "All this — this — taste and color and charm — I never dreamed there was such an oasis of beauty so near."

The dark eyes of his host glowed with pleasure. "You like flowers, Padre? Come, I will show you — oh, no; not now," he said, subduing his enthusiasm. "You are perspiring and it is hot. First, we will take something for your refreshment."

He called out, and in a moment a number of servants appeared. Orders were quietly given. One of the men took the Father's hat and Don Ernesto led the way up a broad staircase.

"You have been very sick, Padre?" inquired Don Ernesto solicitously.

"For several weeks, Don Ernesto."

"You are very pale."

"Dysentery does that to you."

The priest's dusty shoes left prints on the gleaming black of the polished wood. They seated themselves in a large room, which was delightfully cool. No harsh rays of sunlight penetrated here. Don Ernesto's neatly parted black hair showed touches of grey about the temple. His trim little moustache added to his neat appearance. His dark eyes were snapping with manifest delight at the priest's visit. Cool drinks were placed before them by the servant.

"I've just been up a few days, Don Ernesto," began the priest, "and my first visit is, as you see, a pilgrimage of thanksgiving."

"For what? For what?"

"For all the delicacies and medicines you sent while I was ill."

"*Ala! Poca cosa!*" (small matter) ejaculated his host with a depreciating sweep of his hands. But he was evidently pleased. With the simplicity and eagerness of a child anxious to display its toys to another, he stood up and said to the priest, "Would you like to see the house?"

"Delighted, Don Ernesto."

They walked slowly, the compact little host was very voluble concerning his treasures. There were cases of curious coins, delicate bits of carving, vases, elaborate bric-a-brac, chandeliers, some really fine paintings. Don Ernesto had studied both in Spain and in England. He laughingly pointed out two landscapes in oil.

"Why do you laugh, Don Ernesto?" queried the priest. "They are exceptionally good."

His host beamed. "I painted them," he confessed.

He led the priest through a number of elegant rooms, the floors of which were innocent of dust. "During the hot season the *gente de razon* (society folk) come from Manila. Otherwise I am a hermit," he explained. The priest's gaze noticed again the black band about his arm. No one had died here recently, he knew.

When they came to the library the priest felt a warm glow run through him. Books were marshalled compactly on shelves from floor to ceiling, their backs gleaming with some chemical preparation to discourage the depredations of tropical insects. A pair of wide-armed chairs, a spacious table, a box of tabulated cards in a corner. Enthusiastically, Don Ernesto went about, pulling down volumes, discoursing about authors.

Could this be the man of whom Father Templeton had heard so much during the past months from the people? Fields of sugar cane, huge kokals, luxurious home, all these he had, but his main interest was with the village folk. Most of them he knew by name. To all of them he was a paragon, a resort in need, a counsellor and helper in trouble. Not that he was a soft fool. No one was readier than he to finance the construction of a fish corral, or to outfit a fisherman with *banca* and needed equipment, but he knew the man very well before he ventured to assist him. Once assured of a man's industry and uprightness his aid would be quick and generous. The contract never needed paper either. He bore the expense of the outlay; the fisherman did the work. The profit was split equally and Don Ernesto would take care of all repairs to equipment. Not exactly modern, but it was efficient.

The priest looked at the book in his hand and then at the eager, expectant look in his host's generous eyes.

"Well — thank you — Don Ernesto," he said reluctantly. "But I don't know if I will have time to read it. You see I'm trying at present to read a very difficult book, and it will take all my time and energy."

"Oh," said his host disappointedly. "And what is this book?" he inquired politely.

"The mind of my people," he said.

"*Ala!*" laughed the other. "That is not too difficult. You must speak to them of what they know: the sea, the catch, the tides, their small domestic affairs. It is a very small world, yes. But they can talk intelligently, amusingly, interestingly of them."

"Of course, that is their life," admitted the priest.

"It is real to them," said his host. "They know nothing of any other aspect of life. We must make their way ours."

Over a cup of coffee, Father Templeton again probed to elicit the secret of this white man's success among the villagers. "I noticed many times during the dysentery epidemic, Don Ernesto," he began, "that there would be clothes, medicine, food in the houses. When I asked where they came from, the reply was always the same: 'Don Ernesto.'"

His host smiled genially. "The good God has given me more wealth than I need. I could give them much, but I do not think it would be for their own good. A vast outlay of money on buildings, clothes, and the like would not produce a Garden of Eden." He paused and looked fixedly at the table. In a meditative voice he continued as though he were repeating something he had long ago reasoned out and would not forget — "They are happy if they get their living. Why give them a lot of things they know nothing about? It will only create desires that cannot be realized. That will make them unhappy. I love them too much for that. All that they need to pursue their own simple and satisfying sort of life I give them. There is small profit, if any, to me. My repayment is sharing the joys of their endeavour, their company, their trust."

Here was an opening for advice on the project Father Templeton had conceived. Hesitantly he explained his theories as to the cause of the dysentery epidemic. At once he had an enthusiastic supporter. The matter of the inoculations Don Ernesto would personally attend to. As to the new water-supply, he would write influential friends in Manila to assist the priest's efforts.

Late in the afternoon Don Ernesto invited Father Templeton to pay a visit to his wife's grave. As they walked away from the house the priest asked his host how long his wife had been dead. "Ten years," replied Don Ernesto and a gradual melancholy seemed to settle slowly over him. They came to a large, fenced-in enclosure covering several hectares of ground. An imposing mausoleum, some two stories high, stood in the center of the enclosure. Seemingly unaware of his companion's astonishment, Don Ernesto walked slowly past him. The priest hastened to put himself abreast of his host. "Why — why, Don Ernesto," he said in a subdued voice, "this is really magnificent."

No answering gleam of pleasure showed in his host's dark eyes. "I designed it myself," he stated simply. "It is all of concrete. The statues of those large angels at the four corners are marble. They are from Italy."

In silence they ascended the steps of the monument. A low-walled walk went about it. At each corner stood a praying angel. The marble was snowy white, the sculpturing faultless. From the center of the platform rose a domed edifice. Don Ernesto led him inside. A stone altar was in the center and at the side the crypts. The two men knelt and prayed. A small oil lamp burned steadily before one of the crypts.

When they left Don Ernesto seemed entirely sunk within himself. "Padre, will you come and say Mass in the Mausoleum sometime?" he asked.

"Surely," said Father Templeton.

"It is for my wife," added Don Ernesto. "She was very good — and beautiful. But I want her to know that I am always faithful and thinking of her. The Mass is the best way to tell her that."

The priest's gaze fell on the mourning band about Don Ernesto's arm. It was no longer a mystery.

"Shall we go to the beach?" said Don Ernesto. "I know a path that brings us out above the village and we can walk along the beach to the convento." The priest readily assented. During their walk, Don Ernesto spoke of the sadness that overwhelmed him, the loneliness resultant of a consuming love shattered by sudden death. Details, work were powerless to obliterate this. Books, music, painting, work — all were unable to alleviate it. Only when among the people of the sea, or when walking by the sea did he find momentary surcease. Was it that the uncomplaining acceptance by the people of their own hard lot taught him how to accept his? Was it that the sea's vastness echoed the vastness of his own loss? He did not know. All he knew was that the people of the sea and the sea's wide immensity answered the need that was in his soul.

Father Templeton listened in silence. As they came

down to the beach, Don Ernesto paused and drew a few full breaths of the salty air. They turned up the beach in the direction of the convento. "Padre," he said, "when the sea is in a gay mood, wide, blue, the sun playing on the waves, I feel different, happy."

"It has that power over me, too," admitted the priest.

"It is as though God speaks to me," the other continued. "I feel lifted up. I know then that not all is sorrow and longing. But when I turn home the joy goes from me. I have been lifted up in order to be cast down. Like water, drawn from the sea, only to fall again in futile rain. No; not futile," he said, as though correcting himself. "From the falling rain and its sobs of sorrow God builds the perfect joy and beauty for us — a glorious tree, the rice paddies waving with fertile green, the forests riotous with flowers and foliage." He stopped abruptly as though he had found a satisfactory solution.

A delicate breeze moved the palm fronds along the shore and hidden cicadas sent up their whirring song. Don Ernesto held up his hand. "Listen, Padre," he said in a soft voice, "the trees whisper; the cicadas sing." His eyes drifted dreamily over the water's immensities. "It is only man's song that halts. Man wants to be wise. He should just be happy. That is wisdom."

"A wisdom not easy to find," Father Templeton said softly.

No further word was spoken. As they drew near to their destination, Don Ernesto was silent, seemingly intent on the music of the sea. The priest was thinking of the gallants of Old Castile. Their love for the sea had made many of them great. Magellan — who first sailed the circling seas and then died fighting on the strand at Mactan. Love of that sea was bred in the bone of Don Ernesto. Its large ways, its simple ways were his too. To it he could go in his life's deep and abiding loss and find assuagement for his sorrow. In the uplift of its racing tides, he could find comfort for his spirit. "This meeting," thought the priest, "was not an accident. It has design. A lesson," he muttered, "and a parallel."

Don Ernesto's leavetaking was rather formal. *"Muy buenas noches, Padre,"* and he was gone. The priest knew that he had found a friend.

# Chapter XI

1

THE water was silken smooth, cooling, delicious on the skin. Father Templeton stretched out luxuriously and floated. A wavelet washed over his face, and the salt bit into his eyes and water rolled into his mouth. He spluttered and jerked erect, then turned over and began swimming lazily toward Totoy. A thread of fire wrapped itself about the priest's arm. He trod water while he rubbed the offending spot vigorously. He held his arm aloft, but there was no wound or mark of any kind to indicate what had bitten him. But the searing sensation continued.

Suddenly Totoy cried out frantically and thrashed madly for the shore. Stumbling up onto the sand he rubbed his chest like one demented. Ramon, who had been idling on the sand, caught the youngster by the arm. Father Templeton hastened up to them. There were blistered lines all over the boy's chest. The priest looked down at his own forearm and a single white line showed, running about it like a thread. Ramon laughed. "That is the mark of a jellyfish," he explained. They went to the convento and Ramon doused the whimpering Totoy's afflicted chest with vinegar to take the sting out of the burns. He gave the priest a piece of green mango pulp to rub on his burn.

'Toy blubbered a bit. It was a *"castigo de Dios"* because he had called Gracing a "jellyfish" that morning. The priest consoled the boy. Everyone in the village called Gracing *"Jellyfish."* To their mind Gracing was as inert as that sea dweller that floats so languidly through the water.

Musing over the morning's mishap later in the day, Father Templeton found himself wondering if the villagers had had the sharp stinging quality of the creature in mind when they nicknamed Gracing "Jellyfish."

## 2

The hut was a typical Filipino dwelling: picturesque with its nipa roof, practical with its sawali walls and four solid hardwood posts. The floor was several feet above the ground, ensuring coolness in the warm season and dryness in the rainy season. A fisherman stood gaping in front of the hut.

Gracing waddled into view. He stopped the fisherman.

"Tonio?!" he half-greeted, half-questioned.

The man turned quickly. "Oh, Gracing, hello. I was just wondering at that picture."

Gracing followed the line of the man's finger, which pointed to a crude drawing on the outer wall of the house. It depicted a fish hanging over the edge of a basket. There wasn't any artistry in it. The fish's mouth was opened in a most ludicrous manner.

"Did some rascal make fun of you?" asked Tonio.

Gracing's face reddened a trifle. "No. It is I who drew that. Do you not know what it is?"

Tonio scratched his thigh reflectively. "It is a fish — I think — some sort of fish — "

Gracing could not contain himself. "It is the Seal of the Fisherman, ignorant one."

Tonio turned wide eyes on him. "San Pedro was the first Pope," explained Gracing. "San Pedro was a fisherman. So there is a fish on his seal. All the Popes have that as their seal now. You know when you pay the *cedula* (head tax) there is the government seal? Well, there is now the seal of the Roman Catholic Church."

"But why do you have it on your house?" asked Tonio. "You are not the Church."

"Of course not, *loco*. But I am an officer of the Church. I am the fiscal of Santa Cruz church. I am an officer of our Holy Father the Pope. So I am allowed to display the seal."

"O-o-h, I see," said Tonio, "it is like the shoemaker's shop. He has a seal in front too — an old *chinela* (slipper) ."

Gracing cast a glance full of suspicion at Tonio. Was he trying to be flippant? No, it was just that the fool didn't know any better. The self-styled officer of our Holy Father the Pope grunted and entered his dwelling.

Later in the evening, as he was reclining in a chair after a very satisfying meal, a buzz of voices disturbed him. He was trying to make up his mind to go out and see what was the cause of the gathering when a voice cut through the others.

"It is a fish, I tell you — Gracing told me so himself."

(Tonio, that imbecile, breathed Gracing.)

"It's not a pampano," declared one voice eventually.

"The tail is like that of a sardine," added another.

"But the body . . . caray! . . . that is not fish. . . . It is a wild pig with the mouth of a sailfish."

The bantering went on. Suddenly the voices hushed. There was evidently a new arrival.

"Well," finally said the voice, "what do you think? Is it a fish, Lacay Luis?"

The old man's voice came clearly. "Of course it is a fish. But . . . it is not good to eat." A burst of laughter. "Some fish are good to look at, but not good to eat . . . like . . . like a jellyfish."

Gracing roused suddenly. He stalked to the door of the house but the men had moved away and were in the shadows of some palms. He could not shout at them. It did not become his dignity as fiscal. Lacay Luis' voice suddenly came to him. "He eats them and he can draw them, but . . . he cannot catch them."

A slow tide of anger mounted in Gracing's breast.


3


Gracing's office on the ground floor of the convento is a tiny boxlike affair. Almost the entire front of it is open, commanding the steps leading into the convento. A termite-eaten wooden closet encloses the church records. Gracing's table and chair are at the window. He keeps an eye on the passers-by. Most of the fold who have occasion to pass will stop and lift their hats; or, if a woman, she will lift the burden she carried on her head. Some few may stop in for a visit to the Blessed Sacrament.

Gracing's discerning eye can detect a prospective marriage, funeral, baptism, as soon as it enters the plaza. In
his mind the petitioner's financial ability has been gauged
and he is ready with the papers and *derechos* (diocesan
fees) before the visitor ever sets foot across the official
threshold. The fiscal can be awesome to the people, for
the dignity of his office is ever upon him. Nothing pleases
him more than to see how respectful the people can become toward him. He is aware that all this authority of
his is derived from the Church. His devotion to it and
his allegiance is a matter of pride.

That pride had been offended. The Church's dignity
had been upset in the person of its fiscal, and the fiscal
would take measures to restore it. Since the episode of
public criticism of his work of art, he had diligently inquired of each candidate his or her relationship to Lacay
Luis. If he discovered any faintest connection, be it in
the remotest collateral line, he made trouble. The fees
were hard and fixed, difficulties and delays were
manufactured.

This new procedure began to make talk. Eventually
news of the feud reached Father Templeton's ears. The
Christmas season was at hand and the priest was busy
with church preparations. He did not want to get into
this imbroglio. He feared Gracing's reaction and he had
a dread of Lacay Luis' quiet eyes and cold words. But
then, Buff's words came to him: "their troubles. It won't
be easy. Don't fool yourself." Half-heartedly, he went to
Lacay Luis and made a few roundabout remarks on the
subject of the feud. The old man gravely listened and
said, "I do nothing." So he had to go to Gracing. Mindful
of Gracing's nickname, "Jellyfish," he rather feared the

results of a direct approach and puzzled to find a diplomatic opening.

The opportunity came on the day after Christmas. Father Templeton had discovered a most amazing thing. He hastened to Gracing's office. It was an inauspicious moment: the siesta hour. But his precipitate entrance did not disturb the fiscal. Upright at his desk, sleep was fast stealing over him. His lower jaw relaxed, the lip protruded in a pout, the eyes were closed, the head screwed around slightly. He began a variegated series of bows as sleep stole over him. Amused, Father Templeton watched. First, came a few curt nods of affirmation, then the realization of his impending danger and his weakness, finally an heroic acceptance of his fate; his head fell forward till the man's chin was almost touching his chest. Abject humility. A series of short, spasmodic jerks ensued. At each of them his neck protruded further, like a duck making vain attempts to catch an insect on the wing. Crash! His nose met the desk violently. His waking exclamation had not allowed for the presence of a priest. As he saw Father Templeton a deep pink crept up around his eyes. "It is very warm, Apo," he excused. "I fell asleep."

"It is warm," agreed Father Templeton, as he smothered a smile. "Come with me. I have something to show you."

They entered the church, and Father Templeton pointed to the crib. In the straw before the manger, one of his chickens clucked proudly. Gracing hastily waddled forward and dislodged the intruder. He peered into the straw and picked up an egg. "A *pascua* (Christmas gift) ," he exclaimed.

"One not left by the Wise Men," smiled Father Templeton.

When they returned to the house, the egg in Gracing's pudgy hand begot a sudden idea in the priest's brain. He propounded it to Gracing, but the fiscal disagreed. The priest was not to be deterred. A definite command settled the matter. Gracing, still muttering protests, put his *kalugong* on his smooth pate and trudged off in the direction of Lacay Luis' dwelling, carrying the egg in his hand. Father Templeton was sure that Lacay Luis' shrewd mind would grasp the import of the gift, and make a start toward patching up the feud.

"Did Lacay Luis say anything?" probed the priest when Gracing returned.

"Yes, Padre. He is very grateful," replied the fiscal.

"Fine, fine. Did he say anything else?"

"Oh, yes. Many things. The old always —" he bit off what he had intended to say. "His last word was 'the gift of a priest is a blessing to the receiver and also to the bearer.'"

The priest noted the satisfied smile on Gracing's features and sighed — prematurely.

At Mass, the following morning, someone fainted. Gracing hastened to the rescue. Ramon was lifting the person out. Gracing stooped and picked up the unconscious person's legs. It was only then that Gracing saw it was Lacay Luis. They had taken but a few steps when a sudden spasm shot through their limp burden. The feet of Lacay Luis drove like a pair of piston rods into Gracing's stomach. But the gasping fiscal manfully held on until the inert Lacay Luis was outside the church.

After Mass, Father Templeton found an incensed Gracing storming about the sacristy. "It was on purpose, it was on purpose," he ejaculated.

"What do you mean?" asked the bewildered priest.

"Lacay Luis — he did it on purpose — to disgrace me before the people," asserted Gracing vehemently.

"You mean he kicked you on purpose?" said the priest.

"Yes. I saw him open one eye," maintained Gracing.

"You must have been mistaken."

"I am not, Padre, I know."

"But why would Lacay Luis do such a thing?"

"He will revenge himself on me."

"Revenge?"

"Yes. Because he could not eat the egg I gave him. It was rotten."

Father Templeton ran his hand through his hair. The oil he had poured on troubled waters had just caught fire. There was no peace for the priest that day. Gracing breathed indignation and threats. He sizzled and simmered all day long. Father Templeton tried to settle down to the preparation of a sermon. Gracing burst in to tell him that were he the Bishop, Lacay Luis would be excommunicated for what he had done. In despair Father Templeton took his sun helmet and sought out Lacay Luis. Things had to be smoothed over. The whole village would be taking sides before long.

The old man, looking a bit sickly, was seated beneath the buri palm. Father Templeton sat down and inquired as to his health. The truth was simply told: he had had a seizure and had no recollection of being carried from the church. The priest told him of Gracing's unworthy suspicion. The old man blinked and looked a trifle grim. "I will correct his idea of the whole incident," Father Templeton hastened to assure him.

"A fool wants praise and not correction," said Lacay

Luis didactically. After a pause the old man changed the subject. "Did you see the crib of Don Ernesto, Padre?"

"Yes. I did. It was a marvel. It took up an entire house outside the Casa Grande."

"There are one thousand statues," stated Lacay Luis.

"The lights and colors, mountains, rivers, forests — I thought it was very beautiful," said the priest.

"It was better before, when Ramon helped," replied the old man.

"Ramon? Did he help before?"

"Yes; he is very good at that."

"Why did he not help him this year?"

"He does not help him for several years now."

"Why?"

"You do not know?" with evident surprise.

"No."

"I will tell you, Padre." He looked at the priest. "Ramon is the son of Don Ernesto."

"Wh-a-a-t?"

Lacay Luis' eyelids drooped in slow assent. "The only child," he added.

So that was the explanation of Ramon's obvious difference from the villagers: he had white blood in him. "Well, why does he not live with his father then?" asked the priest.

"It is the wife of Don Ernesto that is the cause."

"Why, she is dead," blurted out the priest.

Lacay Luis' eyes drooped in affirmation. "Don Ernesto is good; very good. But he is also loco about his wife."

"Lacay Luis!" ejaculated the priest at the old man's disparaging word.

The old man did not water down his statement. As

though nothing had been said he continued, "She wants Ramon to be a priest. Don Ernesto will do everything for his wife when she is alive. He will do more for her when she is dead. He will make Ramon a priest."

"Yes?"

"But — Ramon does not want to take the priesthood. He loves his father, he loves his mother, he loves the priests. He does not love to be one."

"I see."

"Don Ernesto and Ramon have many quarrels. Then Don Ernesto say if no priest, no son. Ramon must then leave the house. He is no more his son."

Father Templeton sucked in his breath. This revelation of Don Ernesto's character jolted him. Yet, that almost fanatical devotion to the memory of a long-dead wife! Lacay Luis' story explained much.

"Don Ernesto is very kind," went on the old man, seemingly understanding what was going on in the priest's mind, "very gentle, but also very stubborn. And Ramon is the son of his father."

"And now?" prompted the priest.

"Ramon will marry Marita." The old man dropped the simple statement like an irrevocable decree. It swept over the priest like a blast of fire. Knowing so well the mind of Don Ernesto, he sensed to the full what this would mean to the proud haciendero.

"Manolo helped Ramon," went on the old man, unravelling further implications. "So Don Ernesto is displeased with him. The fish corral of Manolo, you see," his arm gestured to the sea, "is gone. The last typhoon took it. Don Ernesto does not even speak to Manolo. How can Manolo rebuild the corral? Up till now Don Ernesto has hopes, always hopes, that Ramon will change his mind. If Ramon marries Marita, there is no hope."

"I understand," mumbled Father Templeton.

"Manolo is *capitán* of the village. The people fear now that if Ramon marries Marita Don Ernesto will be very angry. So angry that not only the *capitán* but the whole village will be without his help."

The old man had finished. He looked steadily on the face of Father Templeton. After some time the priest's gaze met his. "Thank you, Lacay Luis," he said. "I did not know this." What was he to answer? All thought of the petty feud between Gracing and Lacay Luis was now forgotten. This was something more vital. It struck at his own deep interests and those of the village. He could not decide right off. The words came haltingly: "It — it requires some thought."

Unaware of the tempest stirred up in the priest's heart, the old man's gaze followed the slow-moving white figure. There was disappointment in his weathered countenance. He had not thought their conversation would end thus. Did the young Padre not understand their need? Did he not realize that he alone had the power to assist them? He leaned his old back against the buri palm's trunk, shifted his betel quid a trifle, and gazed out over the sea.

# Chapter XII

### 1

IMMOBILE, the youth sat in the cool shade of the bamboos. His face was thin-cheeked, his mouth almost lipless, and his eyes, behind their spectacles, loomed feverishly large and alert. He placed a black, salty sunflower seed between his teeth, split it, dexterously tongued the meat out of the shell, swallowed it, and then sucked on the salty container. Soon he spat it out. A fighting cock tied to a neighbouring shrub pecked curiously at it. He paid it no attention. His eyes were fixed on the river that gurgled past a short distance away. Suddenly they brightened with attention.

A girl came daintily barefooting her way up the rocks of the river. At her side she held a tray heaped with clothes. The sun gleamed on her black hair as she stepped from shadow to sunlight; and she sang as she came. Directly in front of the spot where the man was partly hidden she stopped. Two large flat rocks jutted into the stream. Placing her burden on one of them, she carefully lifted her dress above her knees and sat down on the other rock. For a moment she dabbled her bare feet in the water, then turned to her work. She soaped a garment and began to pound it vigorously with a paddle.

From his vantage point along the bamboos the young man watched the girl intently. She was a picture of loveliness. Slim and with her dark masses of hair coiled on top of her head, she was graceful in every move of this homely piece of work. Absorbed in her work, she had not noticed him. Carefully he took his fighting cock under his arm and sauntered down to the girl.

"Good morning, Marita," he said with an ingratiating smile.

The girl's startled glance flashed over him, taking in the white drill trousers, the *barong tagalog*, the floppy straw hat and the fighting cock tucked under his arm. "Oh . . . Good Morning, Evaristo," she replied, but there was no welcome in her voice.

"You have a lot of washing to do," he ventured.

The girl said nothing.

In no way daunted, Evaristo made another attempt at conversation. "That is the Padre's soutana you are washing, isn't it?" he essayed again.

"What do you think it is?" said Marita scornfully, "my mother's nightdress?"

"I did not know that you did the Padre's washing. Does he pay well?"

"Ask Gracing," came the girl's short rejoinder. "He pays mother." The man was a nuisance. Marita wished he would go away.

"Marita, I am thinking to enter this bird in the cockpit on the fiesta." He held forward proudly the fighting cock.

"It is yours?"

"Yes." Then, after a pause. "There is much money in cockfighting."

"Hmph!"

"You think I do not know how?" he asked sharply, nettled by her contempt.

"O yes, you know how. You knew how to start the school too; and the paper; and the library. You start many things but finish nothing."

Evaristo sulked. "There is no cooperation," he retorted.

"That is not it. You have Manila ideas. This is Santa Cruz."

Evaristo squatted on the ground and began to exercise his fighting cock. He lifted it and threw it sharply to the ground. He held its tail and let it run a short distance; then he held it as it dug its legs into the ground. All this would strengthen the bird's legs.

"It is a good bird, isn't it, Marita?"

The girl vouchsafed no reply.

"It cost me twenty pesos."

The girl said nothing. Discouraged, Evaristo tied the bird by a leg to a tree and broke off a bamboo switch. He seated himself on a rock close to the girl. "Marita, why is it that you do not want to speak to me? Am I not as good as that half-caste Ramon?"

The girl looked up. "Ramon and I will be married. Everyone in the village knows it."

"Yes," came the slow bitter response. "Everyone, also I. But you are Filipina . . . why is a half-caste better than a full-blooded Filipino?"

"Ramon is as good a Filipino as you," she protested vehemently. "His mother was Filipina, and his father is a Filipino citizen who loves us and helps all the villagers in many ways."

"And has a lot of money too," sneered Evaristo.

The girl's face grew red with indignation. "You would not say that if my father were here."

The youth had no answer for that. After a silence he resumed, "You used to speak to me, play, and laugh with me, before I went to Manila. Why did you change toward me?"

"You were different then. You were a good boy. Your studies have changed you."

Evaristo angrily snapped the bamboo switch into the water. "That is the foolishness of all this village. You think that education, that progress makes one no good. You want to live and die catching fish, eating them or selling them. Because I have ideas, I am no longer a good boy," he drew out the last words in scornful mimicry of her.

"That is not so," denied the girl. "Education is good and progress is good. But you are no good for either. You did not finish your schooling in Manila. You bring back ideas ... ideas ... plans ... words. You start one after the other. Like your education, you do not finish any of them. You drink tuba. You boast all the time of how ignorant we are and how wise you are. Can you get married and live on ideas? You borrowed money and did not pay it back. You do not go to church any more. Fishing for everything, you catch nothing. No one has respect for you any more." The girl stopped; her face was red. "You made me angry, so I have told you the truth ... all of it.'

His face torn with conflicting emotions, Evaristo found no words for reply. Angrily, he swished the water with his cane as though to relieve his feelings. How he would have liked to switch the girl instead; this girl who had laid bare all his weakness. He could imagine the yielding water as her soft flesh. He brought the cane down viciously and the water spattered up over the girl.

"Stop that, Evaristo. You are splashing the water over me," she said.

He looked at her steadily. Slowly an insolent grin spread over his hawklike features. An idea had formed in his brain.

2

The river burbled its liquid song of laughter. It flashed joyously over the water-worn rocks, it leaped with gladness in the sunlight, it slid smoothly into the depth of quiet little inlets along its banks.

Hunkered down on rocks at the edge of the water the women of the village were doing their washing. Young girls, matronly housewives. All barefooted, clad in simple wrap-around skirts, leaving their arms and shoulders free. Here and there one of them was washing her long straight black tresses, but most of them were busy thumping industriously the wet clothes with a wooden paddle. They laughed, they gossiped, they flung about Lacay Luis' latest quips and proverbs. Occasionally one cried out a maternal warning to her offspring disporting at the edge of the stream. In Santa Cruz one needed no newspaper. At the public washing all topics of private and public interest were aired, from the birth of a child to the size of the latest patch on a man's clothes.

Father Templeton threaded his way slowly among them. As each of them called out greetings and chatted with him, he found himself harking back to his first visit to this scene. He recalled the evident embarrassment of the women, their reluctance to talk, their attitude of distrust and suspicion toward him. That had all changed now. His visit had gotten to be part of this laundry ritual. If he failed to appear, questions would be asked.

Isabela looked up. She had finished the washing of a garment and with plump matronly fingers was wringing the water out of it. "You are looking for your laundry, Padre?" she queried genially.

"No, Isabela," he smiled back. "Is that my shirt you are wringing out there?"

"No, Padre, that is Ramon's . . . *ai yai!*" She suddenly broke off, "Basilissa, you move away from there! All that soap water is coming down over my place."

"The clothes will be cleaner, Isabela," shrilled Basilissa. "There is more soap."

"Also more dirt . . . go out to that other rock."

"It is deep," teased Basilissa, "and if I fall in I may be drowned."

"Go ahead. The Padre is here. If you drown, we will bury you at once."

The others had been listening, and a general laugh rang out as Basilissa with exaggerated signs of fear nimbly skipped to the new position.

Isabela came back to the subject in hand. "We have a big wash this week, Padre, so Marita is doing your clothes."

"But she is not here, is she?" queried the priest looking about him.

"It is too noisy and she will not be able to finish. The others always like to joke her about . . ." she stopped suddenly and looked up with a curious hesitating glance at the priest.

"About what?" said the priest with pretended innocence.

"Oh . . . Marita is very good-natured. They like to joke with her about . . . things."

"And about Ramon?" added the priest softly.

Isabela's placid countenance suddenly flooded with smiles. "Oh, you knew, Padre, all the time."

He laughed clearly. "Should all the village know and not the Padre?"

"Lacay Luis told you," she guessed.

"Lacay Luis does not know everything," he evaded.

"Everything about the village," came the quick retort.

"Well, now that I know something, too," went on the priest, "I am going to put it to use." He began to move away.

"Where are you going, Padre?" asked Isabela, quickly intrigued.

"To find Marita and tease her about . . ."

"Ah no, Padre," she pleaded.

"About the buttons she battered off my soutana."

Isabela laughed. "That will be good for her. Here comes Ramon. 'Mon," she called out, "take Padre to Marita. She is around the next bend of the river."

The two men walked off, and soon rounded the bend. Thick clumps of bamboo formed a dense screen. They pushed through them, Ramon in the lead. Suddenly he stopped, tense, scarcely breathing. "What is it 'Mon?" the priest asked in a quiet whisper. For answer the youth's arm moved back some of the bamboos. Over his shoulder the priest saw Marita seated on a rock, her paddle falling rhythmically on the wet clothes beneath it. Her head was bent, seemingly oblivious of Evaristo who sat on a near-by rock. There was a whiplike cane in the boy's hand. It flicked the water up and down, persistently, annoyingly, deliberately, spattering water on the girl's neck and shoulders. The boy was watching the girl's face and evidently enjoying the mounting irritation he saw there. Suddenly Marita's head snapped up. "Evaristo, you stop that now."

"Why, I'm not doing anything."

"You are splashing me. Go away!"

"I like it here," came his reply, insolent and designed to aggravate. "And . . . the river is free."

"Oh . . . you . . . you worthless one," she retorted, and angrily picked up a garment, twisted the water from it with a few swift jerks and piled it on the tray with the other pieces of washed clothing. She picked up another garment, soaped it, then began to beat it in the water.

Evaristo grinned impudently. He was making her take notice of him. The water cure was getting results. Deliberately he raised his cane and flicked a flight of cool wet drops at the back of the girl's neck. Like a flash Marita dropped the garment and swung her paddle aloft. It caught the surface of the stream and a sheet of water splashed all over Evaristo. He jumped erect, his spectacles dripping.

"Pest!" he ejaculated, and his face was suddenly contorted. Swiftly he stooped and plunged his hand into the river. It came up with a load of loose mud and sent it scattering over the newly washed clothes.

"Oh . . . you . . ." Marita's tearful voice never finished. Ramon shot between the pair, as though launched from a catapult. His hands had quick hold of the startled Evaristo before the latter knew what had happened.

"You like to play with water, eh?" shouted Ramon, as he heaved the offender into the stream. His strong hands pushed him under and then drew him out. "I like to play too . . ." And he started to put him under again.

"Just a minute, 'Mon," said a quiet voice, and Father Templeton's hand laid hold of his arm. "No need to drown him." Ramon paused. "He might lose his glasses. Go easy."

The priest's quiet words sent the anger out of the boy. He would have liked to drown this rat. He still had hold of him and the temptation was strong. His eyes turned to the priest. Father Templeton suddenly smiled and looked down at his feet. Ramon's eyes followed his. "Padre, you are in your shoes . . . and in the water," he exclaimed.

The priest grinned. "Don't keep me any longer, 'Mon. It's not good for the leather." Ramon grinned back apologetically, his anger completely gone. He released his grip on Evaristo's arm. Swift as thought, Evaristo stooped and plucked a rock from the river bed. Father Templeton stepped quickly in front of him. "You will do no further harm here, Evaristo. Drop that rock," he commanded.

The boy stood irresolute. The priest watching his eyes read his thoughts. "Your glasses are not broken, are they?" he inquired suddenly, solicitously.

With his free hand Evaristo took off his spectacles.

"Come up on the bank," said the priest. They left the stream. Evaristo dropped the rock and carefully examined the glasses.

"No; they are not broken," came the sullen reply.

"That's good. Let's get along now and change clothes. You and I are both wet."

"I don't need you," came the blunt rejoinder. Evaristo

turned and picked up his fighting cock. He tucked it
roughly under his arm. "I'll fix you . . . you peacock
half-caste!"

Ramon had his temper under control. "My skin is a
little lighter than yours," he retorted quietly, "but I am
Filipino. A good one too, Evaristo. And if you are such
a full-blooded Filipino, you should know that we Filipinos do not like to fight, but when we do, we fight
plenty."

"Come on, Evaristo," said the priest placatingly, "let us
get along."

"Not with you," came the malignant retort. "Stay and
protect your pet . . . he is half white." He whirled and
plunged away into the bamboos.

The priest looked at the young couple. "Whew!" he
breathed. "He's kind of hot. Think I'll go after him and
try to cool him off a bit. See you later." He waved a hand
at them and made off after Evaristo.

Ramon picked up the soiled clothes and began to slosh
them in the water. Marita was troubled. " 'Mon, I do not
like Evaristo. I am afraid he will fight with you."

Ramon laughed easily. "He is just a boaster, Chiquita.
I am not afraid."

But Marita was not quieted. "I hope the Padre will cool
his head." She took up her last piece of washing. "Why did
the Padre come here, 'Mon?"

Ramon's gurgle of laughter drove some of the anxiety
from her face. "It was the buttons. He says you break all
the buttons with that paddle."

She paused, the paddle held upright. Dismay spread
over her face. "Do I break them, 'Mon? Really, did he say
that?"

"Sure; and he said that he will not pay you for this wash because you broke so many buttons last time."

She looked such a picture of misery that Ramon broke out in a shout of laughter.

"Oh, 'Mon . . . you are teasing," she chided him.

Laughingly they piled the wrung-out clothes on the tray and Ramon hoisted it to his head. As they made their way slowly down the river, Marita said quite casually. " 'Mon, the Padre is . . . different now, isn't he?"

"Different? How do you mean?"

"He comes to see us more. I think he likes us now."

"Oh, everyone likes you, Chiquita," replied Ramon, balancing himself for a moment on a rock. "But no one likes you as . . ."

"As much as you do," Marita filled in the sentence. "I know that, 'Mon. But that is not what I am talking about."

"It is what I like to hear you talking about, flower of my heart." He sang the last three words.

" 'Mon, behave. I mean the Padre is interested in us. He wants to help us. You see how he went after Evaristo."

Ramon was silent a moment. "You mean that now might be a good time to approach him?"

"Yes, 'Mon. You will go and tell him . . ."

"I will go . . . hm, yes."

"Are you afraid?"

"Afraid?" he echoed quickly. "I am not."

His reply had come too quickly. Marita looked at him out of the corner of her eye. "Very well, then I will go with you."

"But I am not afraid," he protested loudly.

"Of course, not, 'Mon, dear," she said with quiet assurance. "But you may not want to say all the things, or you may forget some of them. If I am there, I can remind you."

He looked at her, and suddenly his heart filled. She knew that he would want her, would need her, but she did not want him to think that she knew it. His hand found hers.

For a while they walked in silence. A pair of gaudy plumaged birds flashed out of the bamboos. The stream gurgled musically. Ramon's lips compressed and suddenly he hummed a tinkling run of guitarlike notes. He began to sing, softly, joyously. It was a love song of Old Castile.

# Chapter XIII

$H$ERE it is, Padre," declared Ramon.

They stopped before the enclosure. A stockade wall of bamboos marked the entrance, where the admission fee was paid. The priest looked hesitatingly about him. "Is it all right if I go in?" he asked.

Ramon looked up at him, mildly surprised. "Why not?"

"Well, I'd like to see what goes on at these cockfights but . . . I think . . . in conversation, Father Connors once said something about them. He left an impression as though they were not good things, but I'm not sure."

"Oh, everyone goes to the cockfight on fiesta. See, there are many people here from faraway *barrios*. C'mon, Padre."

When they entered, they found people milling about: big straw-hatted fishermen, eager-faced old men, exuberant young boys, jabbering, shouting in the hot sun. Ramon, taking the priest's arm, led him toward a group of men who were squatting on the ground. A wordy and vehement quarrel was going on among them. The center of it appeared to be Evaristo. He was declaiming vociferously. His face was flushed, his words wild and slurred as if he had been drinking. He shouted and shook his fist at a thick-shouldered elderly man. The man shrugged and turned. "Antonio?" he said.

Antonio had been squatting at his side, but he jumped
to his feet and launched into a flow of words.

"What is the matter, 'Mon," asked the priest in a worried tone. "Why are they quarreling?"

Ramon laughed. "They are not quarreling, Padre.
They are matching the birds for the next encounter."

"Is that all?" the priest's voice held relief.

"But it is the most important part, Padre," explained
Ramon, "it takes very long always."

Father Templeton's eyes roved around the circle of men
squatting on the ground. Most of them held their fighting
cocks on the ground before them, stroking their feathers,
massaging their leg muscles. But they were all attentive
to the words of the speaker. They freely threw remarks,
quips, rejoinders at him, and all joined in the laughter.
The priest grew tired of waiting. "How long will this
keep up, 'Mon?" he asked.

"It is almost finished now. That man with the big
shoulders and the broad flat face is the Maintainer. Antonio's bird will fight Evaristo's," he announced.

"Well, why don't they go ahead?" came the priest's impatient reply.

"The handicap, Padre," elucidated Ramon. "Evaristo
boasted that his bird is from Manila and has killed six
opponents, so Antonio wants a handicap."

"How can they give a handicap to a fighting cock?"
asked the priest.

"Oh, many ways. Usually with the spur . . . you know
what that is, Padre?"

"No, I don't," confessed the priest.

Ramon bent over and spoke a few words to one of the
men. He handed his fighting cock to Ramon.

"You see this, Padre," he asked pointing to the bird's left leg.

"Yes. It's a piece of triangular wood tied with a thread to the leg. What's that for?"

"I show you," replied Ramon. The youth unwound the string and drew off the piece of wood, disclosing a triangular wedge of thin steel beneath. "That is the spur, Padre. It is sharp like a razor. It is fixed firmly to the leg. The bird stabs with that." He sheathed the spur and returned the bird to the owner. "The left foot is the one with which the bird strikes the stronger. Antonio wants Evaristo's bird to fight with a spur on the right foot. Evaristo will not agree."

With more understanding, the priest gazed on the scene. The men spat, cracked coarse jokes and tried to disconcert the hagglers. A *basi* vendor came around, and his fiery intoxicant contributed to keep everyone in voice and vociferousness. Suddenly Ramon joined his voice to the throng. "Evaristo boasted that his bird is such a typhoon killer that he must now allow a handicap. Right?"

A chorus of assent greeted him.

"Evaristo will not fight his bird unless it has the spur on the left foot. Right?"

Another chorus of assent.

"Well, then, let Evaristo's bird fight with the spur on the left leg and let Antonio's bird fight with a spur on each leg."

The assent was so overwhelming that Evaristo had to give in. He did so with a bad grace and with an evil look toward Ramon.

"Come, Padre," directed Ramon, "we go to the pit."

A short distance away the ground had been dug out to form a circular arena of about twenty square feet. A framework of bamboo formed a platform all around and above it. Ramon found the priest a chair. Spectators crowded in, squatting, sitting, standing, waiting for the birds to be let in. In the meanwhile, the Maintainer walked about the arena. His words flowed like a torrent. In response bets were made and the stakes were placed in his hands. He derived a percentage from the winner for this. The sun poured down making his face gleam with sweat, but it did not cause him to stop. This was for him the golden moment when he could make money. When finally his hands were filled with the wagered money and no further bets seemed forthcoming, he let out a loud ringing shout. At once Antonio and Evaristo entered the arena. Both men were solemn and serious, with their fighting cocks tucked beneath their arms. Antonio, with one hand over his bird's eyes and beak, walked to the center of the ring. Evaristo met him there. Evaristo's bird gave its opponent a vicious jab with his beak. The crowd shouted. Then the process was reversed. Evaristo hooded his bird's head and Antonio's bird had a fierce peck at it. This was to awaken the fighting instincts of the birds.

Each man then set his bird down and carefully removed the scabbard from the spurs. The birds strained at the restraining hands. At a signal the men stepped quickly from the arena. The birds swiftly went to meet each other. Their heads went down and up as though both were activated by one set of muscles. They sparred for an opening. Suddenly there was a flurry of feathers. Antonio's bird flew straight up and Evaristo's went up in the air with it. Evaristo's bird struck sharply with its beak. Antonio's flew halfway around in mid-air and fell awkwardly to the ground. A pandemonium of sound broke loose. Spectators howled for Evaristo's bird to jump in for the kill. Flutteringly Antonio's bird got to its feet and seemingly only a trifle dazed went after its opponent. But Evaristo's bird staggered drunkenly toward the side of the arena and crumpled to the ground.

"What's wrong with it 'Mon," asked the priest. "It's eyes are closed."

Ramon was shouting exuberantly. He turned to the priest. "It cannot see. Antonio's cock slashed it across the eyes in mid-air. *Mabuhay!* I bet a peso on Antonio."

A terrific uproar ensued, and people swarmed into the arena while the winners clustered about the Maintainer. He began to pay off. Antonio shouted a jibe at Evaristo. "Take the bird home and make chicken soup, Evaristo."

The blood congested in Evaristo's already inflamed face.

"It will be expensive soup," jeered the Maintainer, "Manila soup . . . twenty pesos a plate."

Evaristo suddenly saw Ramon. He pushed his way toward him. "You . . . you are the fault, half-caste. It was the spur on the right foot that slashed the eyes of my bird."

"It was a fair handicap," laughed Ramon. "Your bird was the killer of six, Antonio's bird had not even fought."

Evaristo, a crazy light in his eyes, pushed up closely to him. Ramon's hand gave him a shove that sent him backward into a group of men. Evaristo's hand flew to his bolo. Like a covey of startled partridges the crowd flew apart. Quickly the priest ran up to Evaristo.

"Wait a minute, Evaristo, wait a . . ."

"Get out of the way . . . get out of the way . . ." rasped the youth. His face contorted with hate and a wild light in his eye.

"*Amok! Amok!*" came a fleeing person's cry, and with it a chill ran through the priest's heart and involuntarily he backed away.

A hard brown body hurtled through the air and Evaristo fell sprawling. The impact of the unexpected fall shook the bolo from his hand. The priest snatched up the weapon. Ramon and he ran up to the struggling figure. Manolo rolled over and pinned Evaristo prostrate. Never had the priest seen such venom and murderous hate look out of human eyes.

"Some rope," ordered Manolo.

It was swiftly forthcoming and they bound up the struggling Evaristo. "Take him to Lacay Luis' house." Two sturdy fishermen led him off.

Manolo knocked the dust from his clothes. He looked up at the priest. "You must never stand in front of one who is *amok*, Padre. He will kill you," he said simply.

"I just thought he was angry," stammered the priest.

"It was very brave . . . but foolish," said Manolo.

The priest felt foolish and rebuked.

"But it saved my life," put in Ramon gratefully.

"No, Ramon," denied the priest. "Manolo did that. Let us get out of here. I have had enough of cockfighting . . . and of all fighting for a while."

Some hours later Ramon came to the convento. "Will you come to Lacay Luis' house, Padre?"

"Something else about Evaristo?" queried the priest anxiously.

"Yes, Padre. It is a very small village and we have no

police here. We call the Constabulary from Minandang, if anything bad happens. But Manolo and Lacay Luis and the village decided not to give Evaristo to the Constabulary. They will send him away but they want you to see him before he goes on the boat this afternoon."

The priest trudged over to Lacay Luis' house wondering what was to happen. Lacay Luis greeted him quietly. Evaristo sat in a chair, his hands unbound, but Manolo and another fisherman stood vigilantly at his side. The youth was silent.

"Evaristo is leaving the village, Padre," said Lacay Luis. "Before he goes he will beg pardon from you for his behavior this morning."

He looked at the youth. Evaristo's head came up and he faced the priest. The insane light had left his eyes, but in them Father Templeton saw a cold implacable hate.

"I will not beg your pardon," said Evaristo. "You are the cause of all this. I would have had my revenge . . . twice . . . if you had not interfered. I have to go away from my own village. I, a Filipino, must leave because of two people, a half-caste and a white man. But I will come back . . . for the same reason . . . because of you and that half-caste."

The cold deliberate words sent more fear into his hearers than his mad attack of the morning. Lacay Luis shrugged.

"With such a one you can do nothing. He asked to see you, Padre, to beg pardon. You see he will always say one thing and do another. He has no place here. The sooner he is away, the better."

Manolo stepped forward. His quiet words of authority matched Evaristo's bold threat. "We have heard what you said. In return I tell you that the day you set foot in Santa Cruz again the Constabulary will be informed of your attempt to bolo Ramon. There is a place in Manila called Bilibid Prison where they keep young men who try such things. Come; the boat is in."

They filed from the room.

# Chapter XIV

1

FATHER TEMPLETON said his breviary ambulando. The veranda and its view of the sea were conducive to devotion. "*Noctem quietam, et finem perfectam concedat nobis Dominus omnipotens,*" he murmured, commencing the Compline. Since that eventful talk with Lacay Luis he hadn't had many restful nights. The implications of it had struck him like a blow. The villagers had turned to him in their need. His growing friendship with Don Ernesto had been noted. They expected him to use it to avert what was for them disaster.

What was he to do? Face Don Ernesto's hard set will? Risk his friendship with this sensitive, educated man? It had grown to be the one bright spot in a dreary treadmill of routine work among the fisherfolk. It gave him inspiration, and imparted to him courage to carry on his priestly labours. A human prop? Yes, it was that. But one he felt he was now unable to do without. The fear of losing it made him pause.

Perhaps Ramon and Marita would change their minds. At any rate it would be some time before the wedding. Don Ernesto might change his attitude. Patience, the key to all locks. He would wait. Totoy's head peered around the corner of the door. "There is Ramon and Marita here, Faddaire." The priest's finger slipped between the pages of the breviary. Ramon and Marita. So it had come. His procrastination was not to be indulged.

"Send them here, Totoy," he said. He had thought and prayed. Now he must face the issue.

The young couple entered. The freshness of them, the vitality of Ramon, the shy beauty of Marita struck the priest. He gestured to two chairs. The shyness of the about-to-be-married was on them. Mutely they gazed at the priest. It was the embarrassed silence of two good clean souls. A smile spread over Father Templeton's serious face. "Well, Ramon, what is it?"

Ramon gulped a bit. "We will be married, Padre," he blurted out.

The priest looked at Marita. A glorious blush suffused her features. "You have seen Gracing?" he asked.

"Yes, Padre," replied Ramon quickly. "All the papers are made out." He did not look happy about it. The priest looked at Marita. Her face was still blushing and she appeared anxious to speak.

"And now, I suppose," ventured the priest, "you want to change your mind."

"Oh, no, no, Padre," broke in Marita, and then caught herself and blushed still deeper.

"No, Padre," said Ramon in a steady voice, "we will be married."

"Very well then. The *proclamas* (banns) must be announced for three successive Sundays, you know, before your marriage. So we will begin next Sunday."

A look of relief, of pleased satisfaction, crossed the faces of the young couple. Marita's soft dark eyes remained fixed on the priest's face. An unasked question lurked in them. Before it found words, Father Templeton was ushering them, with good wishes, to the door. He did not want that decision now. One thing at a time. To determine to perform the marriage had been a matter that took many a sleepless hour before a decision could be reached.

Sunday evening Father Templeton slowly left the convento. At the bottom of the steps Gracing called out to him. "Yes, Gracing," he said, waiting. The chubby fiscal came out from his office. "You are going to Don Ernesto, Padre?"

"As usual," assented the priest. "It is Sunday evening. Why?"

The fat face of Gracing was covered with a worried look. "This morning, Padre, I read the *proclamas* for Ramon and Marita. I saw Don Ernesto in the second bench. When I read 'The banns of marriage are proclaimed for the first time between Ramon de Hierro y Martinez and Marita Escalante' — Carrambolas! He is like one shot." He ran his palm over his face like a washcloth. "I think he will be very angry, Padre."

"I think he will," agreed the priest.

"You will visit him?" asked Gracing dubiously.

"As usual," said the priest and with a muttered "*A mañana*, Gracing" (till tomorrow), he strode off.

He had to face the issue. As a priest, his duty to administer the sacraments was paramount. He was certain he could make that clear to Don Ernesto. Yet, it was with some trepidation that he entered the Casa Grande. What would his friend think about his failure to speak with him about the matter before publishing the banns?

Don Ernesto hastened down the steps to greet him. His

face was alight with welcome. The priest's anxiety and fear dropped from him. Don Ernesto was at his best. They ate, they chatted, Don Ernesto played the piano. He was the perfect host, gay, hospitable, entertaining. The evening was a great success.

It was only later in the evening, when back in his simple dwelling, that the priest saw through Don Ernesto's bright gaiety. The proud Castilian heart would not bare its wound to another. It would show to his friend that he could laugh even while his heart bled. How stupid he had been! In the sheer relief of finding no vituperations heaped upon his own head, he had given no thought to what Don Ernesto's gaiety must have cost him.

The following morning Marita, fresh, slim, expectant, came to visit him. She was alone. She took but a few minutes before coming to her need. "You went to visit Don Ernesto last night?" she queried.

"Yes, Marita."

She leaned forward, "Father, did Don Ernesto say anything?"

"Say anything? Why — " the girl's expectant attitude arrested him. So that was it. "You mean about the marriage, I suppose?"

"Oh, then, you know, Father?"

"What?"

"That Ramon is Don Ernesto's son."

"Of course. Lacay Luis told me."

Her eyes gleamed with excitement, a slight flush covered her cheeks. "Then you spoke to Don Ernesto? You — you explained to him, Father?"

"Why, no," said Father Templeton awkwardly. The light fled from the girl's eyes. "I couldn't put my foot into that. He doesn't know that I'm aware of the fact that Ramon is his son. In fact, he has never so much as mentioned that he had a child."

Marita nodded dully. "He said when Ramon left the Casa Grande, 'You are now dead to me!'" She looked beseechingly at Father Templeton. He kept his eyes fixed on his breviary and idly thumped it on his knee. "Can you not make Ramon live again for his father?" she pleaded.

"I don't think I can, Marita. I — I don't know how to go about it. Don Ernesto will resent it if I open the matter. He, himself, does not intend to talk to me about it."

"Ramon loves him very much," explained the girl, still with a petition in her voice. "We do not want his father's displeasure on our married life. We waited and waited, but he will not give in." The priest silently kept thumping his breviary on his knee. "Father," persisted the girl, "if God wanted Ramon to be a priest I would not keep him. Ramon did not know me before he left his father's house. He never wanted to be a priest. We are not doing wrong, are we?"

The priest's eyes jumped to hers. "No; of course not. You are both of age. Vocations are gifts of God. One's parents don't give a vocation, you know. Only God can do that."

"Then you will speak to Don Ernesto? Explain to him?"

A harassed look came over the priest's face. "I'm afraid I can't do that," he answered with a shake of his head. "Go ahead with your marriage. If ever the chance offers to speak to Don Ernesto, I will do so."

He had shirked it. He felt that much as he wished to be among the people, he had failed in the task of mediation. The girl understood that as well as the priest. As she left, the pleading look still was in her eyes.

2

Lights flickered gaily against the trunks of the palm trees. The dulcet strains of guitars floated from the nipa-thatched hut. Laughter and voices were loud, for at a marriage feast the tuba cup passes freely from hand to hand. Outside Manolo's house, Father Templeton stood watching Manolo supervise the roasting of the *lechon*. Slowly the dusky-brown men turned the spit. The delicious smell of the roasting pig came to his nostrils. The light of the fire flared. Manolo came over to him. Sweat beaded his brow. "It is hot by that fire, Apo," said Manolo.

"It is always hot for me, Manolo, even without the fire," said the priest. "Your land is not like mine." The priest stopped suddenly. Why had he said that? He had meant the reference to be to the tropic heat, but it had not impressed Manolo that way. They stood in silence, gazing at the flames, each busy with his own thoughts. A burst of loud laughter caused him to lift his eyes to the house. Ramon stood framed in one of the openings used in lieu of windows. His face was radiant with laughter and his voice rose clear as he called a toast to the people in the room.

"You have a fine son-in-law, Manolo," said the priest.

The fisherman turned his slow smile on him. "Yes, Apo," he agreed.

"And you always did have a good and beautiful daughter," added the priest.

"Yes, Apo," and Manolo's slow smile grew a little tender. "You do not care to go into the house, Apo?" he invited.

"Afterwards, perhaps," replied Father Templeton. "I am not much for festivity."

They watched the spitted pig rotate before the fire; its sleek sides were turning a luscious brown.

"How are the plans for that fish pond coming?" asked the priest.

The smile faded abruptly from Manolo's face. "There are no plans any more, Padre," he stared bluntly. His one arm gestured toward the sea. "There is no fish corral."

The priest paused. "Did you ask Don Ernesto about having it repaired?"

"He does not speak to me any more," said Manolo a trifle sadly. "But Ramon wrote a letter to him for me."

"And?"

"There is no answer."

"*Lastima*" (too bad), condoled the priest, but his sympathy sounded false in his own ears. Manolo's clear slow glance had a way of going through one. There was no verbal complaint, but the simple fisherman's feelings were as real and apparent to him as though the words had been spoken. It was as though he had said: Don Ernesto would be here at this wedding feast if you had asked him. But you didn't. You did the least you could. You married them. There was no escaping that, so you did it. You think of your own comfort first, not of others. You feared to offend Don Ernesto. You fear right now that you might lose his friendship. You fear to lose those fine suppers. You fear — fear — fear!

If Manolo had spoken the words outright they could not have cut more deeply into his soul.

"Well, good night, Manolo," he said abruptly, turning and hurrying away.

Manolo lifted a hand as though to detain him and then quickly dropped it to his side. The light from the fire caught a look of surprise upon his simple face.

# Chapter XV

THE months slipped by in a routine of work and same-
ness. Frequently, Father Templeton found himself re-
viewing his strange experience in the church the night
before he had commenced going among the people. It
had shown him so vividly the road he had travelled thus
far. But there had been no indication of this present difficulty. He could recall no sight of Don Ernesto in that
curious fading phantasmagoria of sights. What could it
all have meant? His faith in the genuineness of the experience had grown; he had seen all of the details of it
verified, and now he enumerated them. Suddenly he
stopped. That last one: the man by the jet of water. That
element of the experience had not yet occurred to him.
He shrugged his shoulders. There was nothing in that to
solve the trouble between Don Ernesto and his son.

Ramon and Marita were established in Manolo's small
dwelling. The young couple were happy, but in the girl's
eyes the priest frequently saw that unspoken plea. Ramon
and Manolo never broached the topic to him, but to his
uneasy conscience their silence spoke more than words
ever could. Between Don Ernesto and himself a sort of
tacit agreement had been reached: the marriage had never
been mentioned.

Things were at this unhappy impasse when Totoy

stepped in and innocently enough started the ball of events
rolling.

"Faddaire, we will go shrimp fishing tonight," he declared in that half-questioning voice that was suggestive
of statement, invitation, and request.

"Really," replied the priest. "And who are the 'we'?"

"I and Manolo — tha-a-t Ramon, and you, if you like,
Faddaire."

"Oh, I'm no good at fishing," disclaimed the priest.

"But it is easy, Faddaire," urged the boy. "You do not
go in the boat. They are by the shore. You catch them
with your hand. Like the crabs. You remember, Faddaire?"

The priest smiled reminiscently at that carefree afternoon when Lacay Luis had surprised him, sprawled in the
sand over a crab hole. What had he learned from that
event? The words came unconsciously to his mind: from
present conditions to shape present joys. Lord knows he
needed a little diversion. "All right, Totoy, I'll be with
you," he suddenly agreed.

It was a glorious night, glorious even for the tropics.
The sky was peopled with myriads of gleaming stars. The
tide was at its lowest ebb. Father Templeton rolled his
trousers, fisherman fashion, far above the knees. Dried
bamboos were lashed together into a large bundle placed
on Totoy's shoulder. Manolo ignited the projecting end
of the bamboo bundle. They walked down toward the
sea, over the moist sands, till the water was above their
ankles. The air was balmy, the water silken soft and cool.
Ramon carried a pail. The ruddy glow cast by the flaming
bamboos illumined a wide patch of water about them.
They moved slowly, parallel to the shore, their eyes intent
upon the water. "There!" ejaculated Manolo. A smoky

trail blurred up in the shallow water. It ended up at a small stone. Swiftly Manolo's hand darted beneath the stone and the pail tinkled as he dropped the captured shrimp into it. The fun became fast and furious. Repeatedly Father Templeton brought up a tightly clasped handful of sand and mud, but no shrimp.

The only one of the group who seemed to take no part in the enjoyment was Ramon; he carried the pail but seemed disinclined to take part in the sport. "What's the matter, Ramon?" asked the priest. "You can't miss any more than I do. Join in," he urged. Ramon smiled and shook his head. Manolo straightened up with another shrimp. "Ramon must be serious now. He will soon be a father," and a grin made him look elfish in the flaring light of the torch.

"No?" ejaculated the priest. "Is that so, Ramon?"

Ramon nodded affirmatively. "Soon there will be a baptism," he prophesied.

A grunt of warning caused all to pause. Manolo's bolo came quickly out of its sheath. A flash in the bamboo's glow and then Manolo flicked the still-squirming halves of a water snake shoreward. *"Malo"* (bad), was his serious comment.

"There! There! Faddaire," suddenly shouted Totoy.

Father Templeton jumped. "Where?" he cried out.

Ramon's hand shot into the water and came out holding a shrimp.

"Oh," breathed the priest in relief. "I thought it was another snake."

While they laughed and went on with their sport, a thought kept hammering at the back of the priest's mind. Ramon was to have a child. Here was another chance to approach Don Ernesto. Surely the old man's heart could not hold out any further against his son.

"*Hola!*" came a hail from the beach. With the torch's glare in his eyes, the priest could not at first make out the approaching figure. "Padre?" came the hail. Father Templeton froze. He looked at his companions, each of whom stood quite still. "It is Don Ernesto," said Totoy in a low voice. "*Suerte?*" (luck) questioned the new arrival as he came into the glow of the torch. Then suddenly, as he saw the priest's companions, Don Ernesto stopped. Only the spat and hiss of an ember from the torch as it hit the water broke the silence. But the caballero had himself under control. He turned to the priest. "You have caught many, Padre?" he asked, oblivious of the rest.

"Many," agreed the priest. "Do you want to join us?" he invited, noticing that such must have been his friend's intention, for he had discarded his shoes.

"No," refused Don Ernesto. "The torch is burning low. I just came out to wet my feet with you."

The group walked silently up out of the water. The priest stole a glance at Ramon's face; the young man was looking at his father who was ahead of him, and the longing in the youthful face smote the priest's heart. A wave of anger rode over him. He would speak to Don Ernesto now. He must not be allowed to carry on this senseless quarrel indefinitely.

On the shore they picked up their shoes. "I'll not accompany you, Manolo," said the priest. "I have something to talk over with Don Ernesto."

A gleam of hope shot over the faces of Ramon and Manolo. Silently they turned their backs. At a signal from the priest, Totoy smothered the torch in the sand and scampered after Manolo. He had a liking for fresh shrimp. In silence, the two men brushed the clinging sand from their feet and donned their shoes. They rose and started walking toward the convento.

"You like the beach, Padre?" asked Don Ernesto pleasantly.

"Eh? — Oh, very much, Don Ernesto."

"And the people? You like them too?"

"Deeply," the priest hastened to reply. Here was his opening. Don Ernesto cut in smoothly.

"They are like children, no?"

"Very much so," agreed the priest. "God's children."

"That is true," was the reply. "To enjoy them one must also be a child — a child of God."

"That is a truth which I am only beginning to learn," answered the priest.

"No," denied the other, "it is a truth which I think you already possess. Enjoy their simple pleasures, suffer with them in their sorrows, and come to them eager to learn the great lessons they have learned from the sea."

Father Templeton was puzzled by the conversation. Was his friend just making talk to keep him from broaching the forbidden subject? His voice did not sound exactly that way; it had rather the timbre and half-dreaming quality that had characterized it the first day they had met and had walked along this very shore. The caballero seemed to be very serious. It looked as if he had quite forgotten the fact that he had just met his own son. It was hard for the priest to understand the man's mind; a mind by turns immovable rock and impressionable clay.

The bay was ineffably quiet. Far off on the horizon a shooting star drew its trail of glory across the heavens and vanished in the dark. The peace of tropical night was about everything. Don Ernesto's voice quoted softly " 'He made the universe that you may know him.' "

Father Templeton made no comment on the apt quotation. He thought he understood this new mood of Don Ernesto. The unexpected meeting tonight had opened the wound caused by his son's defection, and he had had recourse to the lessons of the sea to salve the soreness of his spirit.

"*Muy buenas noches,* Padre," said Don Ernesto as they reached the convento. Then he was gone.

The priest had let his chance to speak slip by. Weariedly he entered the convento. It was dark and deserted, quite in harmony with the dejection that lay heavy on his soul.

# Chapter XVI

## 1

THE detonation rumbled and quivered across the bay. The priest awoke at the sound. He noted it, half consciously, and thought it a clap of thunder. Sleep was heavy on him. He lapsed back into slumber.

He was late for Mass and hurried through his breakfast. The fleet would be in. The sun was bright overhead, the ground dry as a bone. He paused and with one shoe scuffed the surface. It had not rained. Had not a clap of thunder wakened him early that morning? Evidently the cloud must have passed off to sea. Eagerly he strode toward the beach. This had grown to be a ritual with him. He found fresh cause for wonder in the pleasure which the society of the simple good folk afforded him. Some coins jingled in his pocket. This morning he was going to bargain for a day's fish. 'Toy had given him very minute instructions. He was sure he would enjoy this.

His free-swinging stride suddenly stopped. A puzzled look spread over his countenance. The boats were there, the beach, the sea — but nothing else. Stupidly, he looked about him. Something had happened! He began to run toward the village. Why had they not called him? He threaded his way through the palm trees and found the dusty road. Before Manolo's house a number of women were talking volubly. He hurried up to them. They arose and greeted him.

"What is it, Isabela?" he asked a trifle breathlessly of Manolo's wife. "Has anyone been hurt — killed?"

Her placid countenance remained undisturbed. "No, Apo. It is the Japanese."

"Japanese?" he echoed.

"Last night they dynamite," she said prosaically.

Through the priest's mind flashed the memory of that detonation that had broken his early morning slumber. He cast a wide ranging glance about, seeking the spot of the destruction. "Where — where is the place they dynamited?"

Isabela's broad countenance broke in a faint smile. "It is not the house they dynamited, Apo — it is the sea."

"They blew up the sea?" ejaculated the priest incredulously.

"Yes. That kills the fish," she explained patiently . . . "many of them, thousands of them."

"Apo?" said a quiet voice at his elbow. He spun around to face Manolo. Manolo had left the door ajar when he came out of the house. A hum of voices came to his ears. There must be a meeting of the men there.

"Manolo," said the priest. "Isabela just tells me that the Japanese have been dynamiting your fish."

The swarthy little *capitán* nodded. "They have a big motorboat. It is over there. Come, I show you." He led the priest back to the beach and gestured to the section of the bay beyond Magdalen reef. The priest's eyes picked out the tiny boat, distant though it was.

"They sneak in last night and use the dynamite." Manolo was bitter, and the priest did not know what to say. He had no knowledge of these things.

"Is it — is it bad?" he finally ventured.

"It is not allowed," said Manolo, "not even for us Filipinos. It kills too many fish and drives the rest away. Then there is no food for us."

"Oh, I see," said the priest. This wasn't just bad, this was a catastrophe.

"The Japanese have no right here. These are our waters. But always they come sneaking in. They are going now," he pointed to the boat in the distance, "but they do not fool us. They will hide today and tonight they will dynamite the fish and fill their boat. And then they will go away and for months we have not enough fish to eat."

"Well, why don't you tell the authorities in Manila? The coast guard will put a stop to that."

Manolo shook his head. "When Manila comes, the Japanese are gone. They are very tricky. There will be many of them at different places fishing. The coast guard cannot watch all the bays and islands in the Philippine Islands."

"Well, what can you do? You can't catch their motorboat, can you?"

Manolo's head slowly came down as he thought. "No-o-," he said reflectively, "we cannot catch the motorboat. But — "

"But?" prompted the priest as the *capitán* left the word hanging in air.

"We will have a plan for tonight," evaded Manolo.

The priest turned to him, all eagerness to aid them in whatever way to combat this menace. Manolo's eyes met his in a long curiously impersonal stare. It was not distrust, yet, it was a refusal of his assistance. It was pointed, plain. The priest's eyes wavered and fell. Didn't they want him? Didn't they trust him?

"There — there is a meeting in your house, Manolo — now?" he essayed again.

"Yes, Apo. Lacay Luis is there. He has fought these Japanese many times. He will show us what to do."

Dismissal. That's what it was. Had his efforts among them not merited this much trust?

"Adios, Apo," said Manolo softly. The priest, finding himself alone, felt piqued, offended. The enumeration of all he had done for them these past weeks flowed through his mind. The sick, the visits, the — Marita and Ramon! He had shirked that. Evidently, one was not of the village unless he gave complete allegiance. Manolo was right. After all, he had deserted them in a trying need. What right had he to expect their confidence and trust in an even greater one? Curious how deep was their sense of values and yet, too, how just. But he would show them that he was worthy of their trust; that he was whole-heartedly one with them. He hastened to the convento.

Half an hour later a *banca* slipped quietly away from the shore. 'Toy at the sail looked pridefully at the priest seated in its prow.

"I will make it fly, Faddaire," he gaily announced and, true to his word, the light craft soon careened swiftly for the open sea.

2

Father Templeton looked at his watch. "It's siesta hour, 'Toy," he shouted above the swish of the water and the slapping of the outrigger.

"No siesta, Faddaire," yelled back the boy. He spread one hand out in a comprehensive gesture as though to say there was too much of life for sleeping — water, glorious sun, and breeze, fresh and buoyant.

The *banca* was driving into the bay and the priest found his heart high with the thought of a well-filled mission. He looked about for the Japanese boat. It was nowhere in sight. Had he failed? Would the help come too late?

They were driving right for the shore and suddenly 'Toy shouted. "Many people, Faddaire!" The priest's eyes focused. There were many people. What were they doing on the beach at this time of day?

The boat dropped its sail and Manolo waded out to them. 'Toy jumped out and they began to push the shallow craft up onto the sand. "Manolo," asked the priest, "the Japanese, are they gone?"

Manolo shook his head. "They are hiding over there." He pointed to a piece of the distant bay's shore line.

"Good," breathed the priest. "Now they will get caught."

When the boat grounded, the priest drew Manolo aside from the crowd.

"I went to Father Conners', Manolo. There is a telegraph there. We finally got Manila. One of the cutters is near Minandang and will be here any hour. You must go out in the bay and signal them where the Japanese boat is."

"The Japanese boat is sunk," came Manolo's blunt response.

"Sunk?" echoed the priest, his face a picture of blank amazement.

"Yes, Apo." He made room for Lacay Luis who had

edged up to him. "The Japs have only their little row boats over there. I will go out and meet the cutter and show them." He walked quietly away.

Lacay Luis' chuckle broke in on his amazed silence. "What . . . what happened while I was away, Lacay Luis?" he asked. "Tell me — quickly," he urged.

But the old man would not be hurried. He squirted some betel-nut juice onto the sand and then fixed the priest with a very knowing, owlish gaze. "The Japanese is wily, like a snake. Poison is killed with poison. We are poor but we are not powerless."

"Yes, yes, Lacay Luis," broke in the priest impatiently. "But what have you done?"

The old man hunkered down comfortably and as he spoke his fingers drew vague diagrams on the yielding sand. "Yesterday afternoon, Manolo and Ramon went across the bay and hid." He looked up at the priest. . . . "Over there." His finger pointed across the bay, then drew a line in the sand. "When the Japanese motorboat came, they waited. After a while all the rowboats went off from the ship to start dynamiting; then Ramon and Manolo swam to the motorboat and put dynamite in it, lit the fuse and swam back. The motorboat blew up."

"But . . . but you killed them, Lacay Luis?"

The old man shook his head. "There was no need. All of them were away from the ship."

"But if some had stayed?"

"Ah, if . . . if! Then we would have done something else. Something priests do not allow."

"Was . . . was that why you did not want me at the meeting?"

The old man's eyelids drooped in silent affirmation.

"Your cutter is coming," he said, and pointed off to the speck that moved swiftly into the bay.

"It was very wise what you did, Padre," said the old man, and the palm of his hand smoothed away the lines he had etched in the sand.

The priest looked quickly at him. "You mean getting Manila to send the cutter?" The old man nodded.

"It doesn't seem to have been of much use. You had settled matters already." There was a trace of bitterness in his voice.

"About the motorboat . . . yes," agreed the old man. "We settled that. But about those . . . those slant-eyed snakes . . . we did not know. Some wanted to use the bolo . . . that is not good. Now all is well. They will be taken to Manila and be punished. It is better so." He looked up at the priest and his eyes held quiet gratitude and commendation in their depths. A tiny glow of satisfaction was enkindled in Father Templeton's heart. He had done something, and it was appreciated. It was the village, he knew, that spoke through the voice of Lacay Luis.

# Chapter XVII

FATHER TEMPLETON, leaning against a palm tree, looked upon his work and thought that it was good. It was not much to look at: a flat piece of concrete, rising about six inches above the ground level, with a plain piece of iron pipe projecting from the center of the square. But from that pipe poured a steady stream of clear water. It was the completion of a great effort on the part of the priest.

It had taken a lot of work to get that artesian well dug and the water piped down here. Nestling beneath two large palms in the very center of the village, it was a miracle of the first class to the village people. To the priest it meant the end of the dysentery epidemics and their tragic infant mortality. To the village people, it meant clear fresh water and no long trips to the river for it.

But it meant even more, and Father Templeton's face broke out in a smile as he realized it. A comfortable looking house mother appeared on the scene, a basket of clothes on her head. A little rockpaved canal led off the water from the well. She industriously set to work pounding her washing on the cement. Others speedily joined her. This was good. Village gossip flew about fast and furious. There was the wet sloshy sound of cloth hitting stone. It was good to behold, and the priest found a queer feeling of warmth and satisfaction in silent contemplation of it.

Work, worry, difficulties. These were the coins that paid the price. Sacrificing self for others brought a reward. This ability to be happy at others' joy was a new sensation to him.

A stocky fisherman, his face all smiles, came to get a drink at the well. A cocoanut shell cup was thrust forward and filled with the clear cool water. The man drank thirstily, for he had been working hard. His audible sigh of satisfaction reached the priest. The fisherman tossed a word of greeting to the *lavenderas*. As he turned to leave, a disreputable figure confronted him. A battered straw hat pulled low on the face, filthy shirt and tattered long trousers, a decrepit stick on which he leaned heavily. Father Templeton saw the fisherman pause a moment and then, as though in response to the vagrant's request, reluctantly extend the cocoanut cup. In clumsy eagerness the vagrant lurched forward to seize the cup with his free hand. His bare foot encountered the wet cement. The legs shot from under him. His cane flew from his hand. With a horse cry he fell heavily on the ground and lay outstretched.

Father Templeton darted forward to be of help, but suddenly froze in his tracks. With a shriek, one of the women had arisen and pointed an accusing finger at the fallen man. The fisherman jumped to one side, seized a stick and began to push the helpless creature from the cement. Something snapped inside Father Templeton. The next thing he was aware of was the fisherman's hot breath in his face and his own hands tight on the corded brown arm.

"Take it easy," he was saying. "What is wrong?"

The fisherman ceased his struggling. His eyes found

the priest's. Sanity returned to him. His arm and the threatening stick fell to his side. "That one is leper, Apo," he said.

The priest felt as though his heart had missed a beat. Slowly he faced about and looked at the man, still lying prone on the wet cement; the creature's hat had fallen off and disclosed a haggard face with all the misery of the world looking out of two young eyes. The priest's eyes were fixed but a moment on this. Staring up at him was an abomination of corruption. In falling, the pants leg had pulled up, disclosing a fetid pulp of pus-oozing rottenness from ankle to knee. A wave of apprehension swept over the priest. He flicked his eyes swiftly away to the man's face. No, not a man. A mere boy. The eyes were fixed fast on him.

"Padre," he whispered, "water."

Father Templeton, glad of the respite, swung his back on the petitioner. "He only wants a drink," he said to the fisherman.

"But he is leper," said the fisherman.

"That is no reason to beat him. Aren't you a Christian? Haven't you any pity for him? Just look at him."

He faced about, but the leper's eyes were closed. Quickly the priest went up to him. The boy had fainted. He called out to one of the women. Cautiously, she approached. "Give me some water," ordered the priest.

She did not move. Gingerly she drew nearer, peering the while at the unconscious figure.

"Ai yai!" she suddenly yelled, "that is 'Dolfo!"

"Rudolfo?" queried the priest. "Who is that?" The fisherman drew near. "It is so, Apo," he stated after a glance at the face. "I did not see his face under the hat."

"Well, who is he?" asked the priest shortly.

"He is from here," said the woman hastily. "Some years ago he runs away to the Visayas. All his relatives are dead. He wants to work there."

The cup of water was brought. Slowly the priest sprinkled the boy's face. The fisherman kicked the boy's cane within reach of him, then filled his cocoanut shell with water and set it down beside him. "Drink," he said, "and keep the cup."

"You are Rodolfo?" asked the priest as soon as the boy was revived.

The leper withdrew his drawn face from the cocoanut shell. Water ran raggedly over his dust and dirt-smeared chin. "Yes, Padre." There was the look of a grateful dog in his eyes. "I am sick."

"We understand that, Rodolfo," replied the priest. "Sit down in the shade of that tree — you can walk?"

"Yes, Padre."

"Well, sit down over there till I see Manolo and arrange something for you." A curious hush fell over the group as the priest left.

Manolo had been night-fishing. Roused from sleep, he scratched his head on hearing of the incident. "I will go to the Sanitary Inspector, Padre," he said. "It must be reported. Rodolfo will have to go to Culion. It is the law. We never have lepers here."

Father Templeton went back to Rodolfo. The lad was seated beneath the tree, his leg now covered.

"Rodolfo, you are from this village?" he said standing before him.

"Yes, Padre."

"You know what your sickness is?"

The boy's eyes looked up at him and two slow tears formed and rolled down his wasted cheek. "Yes, Padre."

"Tell me what happened?"

It was a brief recital. Tragedy usually is. He had found work in the Visayas, but the sickness had broken out on his foot. At first it had only been a swelling. He had put many medicines on it. One day the fear came of what it might be. Time changed the fear to assurance. He knew he must die. If the doctors found out, he would be sent away. He wanted to die among his own, near the sea. Often he had dreamed of coming back to Santa Cruz rich and important. Now he had crawled back, a wreck. For the first few days he had stayed in the hills. Then he had no more food. The leg was worse. He had fever. His mind had not been very clear. He was sure his own people would help him.

"They certainly will help," the priest hastened to assure him.

The interview was interrupted by the arrival of Manolo who called the priest aside. He said that the boat for Culion would not call for weeks. In the meanwhile they would care for the sick man. The village would do that. He was one of their own. Manolo speedily had things arranged. A small unused hut at the edge of the village would be the sick man's dwelling. Father Templeton would arrange for clothes and medicine, the village for the man's food.

Manolo sat down beside the priest and explained to Rodolfo how they would care for him; he emphasized the need of his remaining away from the others. Then the priest and Manolo walked with the leper to his new abode. It was a very slow progress. Rodolfo asked them to forgive him but his feet were painful. To Father Templeton's query he replied that both feet were affected.

Gratefully the youth entered the house assigned him. "I hope I die before the boat takes me to Culion," he said simply.

Back at the convento the priest hastily routed out Totoy and explained about the sick boy and his needs. Together they unearthed some old clothes, some bedding, and household utensils. Father Templeton added a bottle of aspirin tablets for the fever. "Now, Totoy, you put all this in the doorway. Don't go in the house, and don't touch anything."

"Yes, Faddaire."

"Explain about the aspirins and then leave them with the other things."

"Yes, Faddaire. Can I talk to him?"

"Of course. But do not touch anything about the house. You may get the disease."

When Totoy, staggering under his burden, had left the house, the priest sat down and drew a handkerchief across his forehead. It had been a very warm day and the unusual experience had come out of a blue sky. A sudden thought flashed across his mind. He held out his hand. It was steady as a rock. Miracle of miracles! Just that first nauseating shock at the sight of the diseased foot — but he had not run! He had done the proper thing! A thrill of self-satisfaction ran through him. And he had thought that the sight of the well and its benefit to the people was a thrill. Why it was worlds apart from this feeling! A feeling of mastery, the ability to meet eventualities and to dominate them flowed over him.

It was strength, fortitude, a sense of having something

within him that was eager to meet obstacles and overcome them. Whence had this sensation come? Out of the
dim past of catechism days his mind began pattering a
stream of words: wisdom, counsel, understanding, fortitude — he stopped abruptly. That was it — fortitude —
a gift of the Holy Spirit. Vaguely yet compellingly there
welled up in his soul the assurance that this was the answer to it all. And with it came the realization of the truth
of the Master's saying: "My grace is sufficient for thee."
Oh, indeed, the long fight had been worth this.

A loud hail flung him back to earth. Father Conners
was laboring slowly up the sand. Eagerly he dashed out
to meet him. This was all that was needed to make the
day perfect: a friendly ear to listen to the tale of the revelation that had suddenly come to him.

"Buff!" he greeted him enthusiastically.

"Hi, Frank! You look like Gaudete Sunday. Feeling
good?" replied the other taking in quickly the evident
happiness radiating from him.

"Swell! Why the unexpected visit?"

"A load of stuff coming in on the boat for me tomorrow.
And I thought I'd get down and be sure they discharge
all of it here."

"You'll stay till tomorrow evening then?"

"Oh, I'll take an extra day besides. I'd like to practice
up on English for a day or so. Have to write a letter home
soon, you know," he added whimsically.

When the guest was established in a *mañana* chair,
Father Templeton told him the tale of the afternoon's
adventure. The elder priest listened to the recital and
at its close his commendation was brief.

"You handled that nicely," he said.

"Oh, that! That doesn't mean a thing. But, Buff, outside of that one bad moment when I first glimpsed the leper's leg, I had no inclination to run, no funny feelings — I — I wasn't afraid."

"I noticed that fact all through your recital," said Buff quietly. "Maybe the medicine is taking hold."

"I know it is," said Father Templeton earnestly. "This going among the people has done a great deal toward helping me."

Buff leaned over and placed a hand on the younger man's knee. "This has helped, too," he said.

"This?" asked Father Templeton, gazing at the knee whereon his friend's hand rested.

"Sure. The prayer bone."

Father Templeton's face was serious as he replied. "I know that, Buff. I wasn't discounting prayer. It was prayer that showed me the way and gave me the strength to walk it, but it is something that I don't feel worthy to talk about. Not prayer, you know, in the sense of petition. It wasn't something I asked for, Buff. I don't quite know how to say it, but it was something that came to me unsought, something that was given to me as an outright gift."

The two priests sat in silence for some time, that curious silence that comes over two people whom friendship has linked together. The evening was wondrously still. A gossamer haze clung to the pitted slopes of the mountains above the sea. Gradually the feeling of elation slipped from Father Templeton and in its stead came the sense of a new trial to be faced.

"Buff," he suddenly said, "your coming is opportune. We have a big affair coming off tomorrow night. You care to take part?"

"What is it?" was the matter-of-fact reply.

"A village celebration for the new well. And also a christening."

"Hm! Kind of a double of the first class," smiled Buff.

Father Templeton's serious aspect did not change. "The christening takes place tomorrow morning. Manolo's first grandchild," he elaborated.

"Manolo's?" queried Buff, his blue eyes suddenly wide.

"Yes, you know that Ramon and Marita are married," said Father Templeton. "Give me some advice on this matter, Buff. Here's the setup." In a few words he sketched the tangle existing between Ramon and Don Ernesto, as well as the complications that had arisen for Manolo and the village. "What am I supposed to do about this, Buff? I need Don Ernesto's friendship. To me, those weekly visits to his house are an oasis in a desert of drudgery. I fear my broaching the matter will not only be useless, but will at the same time destroy our friendship. For all his generosity and lovable qualities, Don Ernesto has been harder than flint in this matter. On the other hand, Manolo, all the people, look to me to present their case. In particular, they want him for the christening tomorrow night. If he can be prevailed upon to come, they feel sure that their gratitude for his help in erecting the well, as well as the sight of his own grandchild, will break down all barriers built up by his quarrel with Ramon. I cannot see what to do. It's one of those involved problems, you know. What would you advise?"

Buff's eyes came back from their view of the bay, and fixed upon Father Templeton's worried face. "It's all quite plain. You don't need my advice." He rose slowly. "You have something now to guide you that I could never give you, my boy. In your present state, my advice would be an impertinence. Well, good night, Frank," and he disappeared inside the house.

The hot blood flooded the young priest's face. It had been a rebuff. For a long time he sat silently gripping the arms of his chair. Then slowly he went over the words he had spoken to Buff, and the strange feeling came to him again that he was not alone. Resolutely he entered the house, sat at his desk and took paper and pen. His eyes stared vacantly at the crucifix on the wall. An opening phrase came to him, another. Swiftly he bent over the desk and began: "Dear Don Ernesto: . . .

# Chapter XVIII

THEY were starting the fires for roasting the *lechon*. From the doorway of the leper's hut Father Templeton could see the huts near by gleaming in the golden light. As the flames swayed and flared, the shadows of the trees danced. Manolo had ordered all the cooking to be done at this edge of the village. It is so easy for fires to start, with the children playing about and the houses so close. It would need but a spark on those inflammable nipa roofs to start a conflagration.

The priest turned back to the hut. 'Dolfo's condition was worse. The reaction had affected his other leg and he could not move. Both limbs were now frightfully swollen and the leper was glassy-eyed with fever.

"Would you like some *lechon*, 'Dolfo?" asked the priest.

"No, Padre," said the youth haltingly, "I — am — very sick."

"Here are the aspirins, 'Dolfo, and the water."

"*Dios ti agnina, Apo.*" (God repay you, Father.)

"Apo — !" called a voice.

The priest left the hut. It was Manolo. They walked toward the beach. After the fetid smell of the leper's house, the clean air of the bay was sweet. Deeply the priest filled his lungs. The silence that lay between the two men was weighted with significance. Their minds were busied with the same thought. The priest looked up finally and put it into words.

"Has Don Ernesto come yet?" he asked.

Manolo wagged his head discouragedly from side to side. "No, Padre," came his quiet response.

They stopped and Manolo faced the priest. "Don Ernesto would not come to the marriage of his son. He would not come when his grandson was born. But Don Ernesto is a good Catholic. Maybe if you tell him today his grandson is born again — Catholic — he will come." He paused as though gathering his forces for a leap. "If you go and ask him, he must come."

"Very well," came the priest's unexpected and ready response. Abruptly he turned on his heel. Manolo in quiet satisfaction watched the white figure swinging up the beach. Suddenly, he turned and raced to the village. A word to several waiting men and the village began to throng about Manolo's dwelling. Men, women, children, yapping dogs, were still straggling in when Manolo arose and addressed them. The Padre had gone to Don Ernesto to try to bring him to this celebration. Now all of them were going to follow with Manolo, Ramon and Marita at their head. Their united appeal was to back up the priest's request. The Padre was to be the wave heralding the approach of the wall of water that subdues all before it. The entire village moved forth as one.

Father Templeton had been so sure that his appeal, delivered by note to Don Ernesto that morning, would succeed. How could Don Ernesto be so stubborn? The priest's mind kept turning over the carefully worded phrases of his letter, the expectation of the village people, the sadness of Ramon and Marita, the anxiety of Manolo.

He was in no quiet frame of mind when he walked up the gleaming black staircase of the Casa Grande.

Don Ernesto came forward to greet him, hands outstretched, his face smiling welcome. Father Templeton ignored the proffered chair.

"Don Ernesto," he blurted out, "you have received my note this morning?" The smile dropped from the hidalgo's face. The lower lip formed a straight line beneath the trim moustache. His figure grew rigid. "Yes; I did, Padre."

"And — ?"

Fire flashed in Don Ernesto's eyes. His words came with inexorableness. "There is no answer." Don Ernesto's face was set like stone.

The priest drew a breath. "I am here, in person, for an answer," he said.

"To you, in person," snapped Don Ernesto, with rising anger, "there is no answer."

Father Templeton's face reddened. Suddenly the words came, deliberately, bitingly, rapidly increasing in tempo as his emotion dominated his control. "Don Ernesto, I wrote you as a friend. I came here and spoke to you as a friend. Now I speak to you as a priest. How you can reconcile your conduct with your own conscience I do not know. But I tell you this — you are doing wrong, grievous wrong. You are not acting as a father to your son. Your conduct has no excuse. It is neither the way of a father nor of a Christian. In this matter it is not God's will you are seeking but your own. God blessed you with a son. Ramon is a clean, good Catholic youth of whom any good Catholic father should be proud. Your wife desired him to be a priest. What Catholic mother does not desire that dignity for her son? It was hers to desire, it is God's to give.

God has not granted it to your son. You, greater than God, dare to bestow it. But God's ways are inevitable and your decision comes to naught."

The hidalgo stood immobile. Father Templeton paused for a moment for some word of reply. No reply came.

"Your son is to you yet an outcast," the priest resumed. "Why? Because God's will in his case has been fulfilled? No. Because your will over his destiny has been frustrated. For that you make others suffer along with him. I say to you, this is pride, stubborn, blind pride. All the time you nourish a ceaseless love for your wife. Loving her whom you can no longer see, and rejecting him, the pledge of her love, whom you have daily before your eyes." He stopped, his eyes flashing, the blood hot in his cheeks. "Ask yourself in your blindness one question: 'Would my dead wife have desired me to treat our son this way?' You have done these evil things from love of her. Her love for you is sure to show you what compensation you can make for the unholy things your pride has led you to do."

For some moments after the priest's sudden departure, Don Ernesto stood like one stricken. Never in all his life had a man ever dared to speak to him like that. The blood pounded in his ears. The hot words of the priest had poured over him like a flood of lava, searing, burning down to the marrow of the facts, pounding on his heart and brain. He slumped into a chair, seeing himself as the priest portrayed him. Father Templeton's impassioned words had torn away the false barriers he had erected about his conduct; his injustice and hardness stood revealed in all its appalling harshness.

Stunned, he sat there. Gradually noises intruded themselves. Voices, the shuffling of feet, the sounds of many people. He went to the head of the stairs. A huge crowd stopped surging upward and froze at attention. Don Ernesto's eyes swept them. Manolo, Ramon, Marita — the whole village. His mind swiftly leaped to the truth.

"All here, eh? — all," he said in a dull voice. Slowly he came down the steps, his neat-groomed, imperious hand sliding slackly over the polished bannister. "You forgot only one thing — Manolo. Where is the baby, my grandson?" The throng parted. He walked slowly through their midst as though unaware of them and so out into the dark of the tropic night.

# Chapter XIX

FATHER TEMPLETON strode rapidly away from Don Ernesto's house with no particular place in view. Soon he saw that he had unconsciously taken the short cut to the beach shown him by the hidalgo on the occasion of their first meeting. He recalled the confidences that Don Ernesto had shared with him that day. The peace he had found in his presence. The joy at the realization of a kindred soul at his side. That friendship had been like the comforting heat of a warm fire on a chilly day; a glow to keep his soul warm in the cold deadly days of routine work. The fire was quenched now. No spark remained, and his had been the hand that quenched it.

Slowly he went toward the beach. He had no fine feeling of having done the right thing. His sharp hot sentences to his friend flashed back into his mind. He had not really meant to speak that way. His feelings had carried him away. It had not been courage. The same things could have been said dispassionately, earnestly, and perhaps would have had more chance of achieving their end. Now he could see in it all just another failure due to a fear of attempting a courageous deed.

The sand was soft underfoot. A curious, dead breeze was abroad. The air was possessed, ominous, like a snake poised to strike. It but added to his already dejected state of mind, bringing as it did a sense of oppression, of danger. As he plodded on toward the village, he became aware of two things: a flare in the trees at one end of the village and a soft slithering sound behind him as of a footstep. He found himself running toward the village. It must be a fire. Manolo's words of caution to the men tending the fires for roasting the *lechon* came back to him. It was a fire! But why the unearthly stillness? Were they all dead? A hoarse breathing at his side caused him to turn.

"The child — where is it, Padre?"

They were in view of the fire now and the priest saw Don Ernesto's face peering up at him in anxiety and fear. The priest's heart gave a great exultant leap. Don Ernesto had followed him! "In Manolo's house," he gasped. "Where are the people?"

"At the Casa Grande," Don Ernesto answered. Here at the edge of the village, where the *lechon*-roasting had been in progress, the fire was blazing fiercely. Flames billowed and danced, forming a raging backdrop of orange light. The trunks of the palm trees stood out like black sticks. A light breeze from the sea was carrying the blaze toward the main part of the village. The breath of the fire reached him, and he shivered as if with fever. Like a bolt the thought of 'Dolfo the leper struck him. He heard a strange whisper "Merciful God!" and then he was running, running madly down to the sea tearing off his cassock. He sloshed the garment in the water, then threw himself flat in the coolness of the sea.

Dripping, slipping on the sand, he charged up the beach, running directly to the spot where the leper's house had been. Tongues of flame flickered out at him;

orange, red, avid tongues that ate to the bone what they touched. Showers of sparks and searing particles filled the burning air. Across the threshold of the blazing hut lay a prone figure. Quickly the priest tore the wet protecting cassock from his own head and wrapped it about 'Dolfo. He picked up his burden. The steps leading to the hut crashed beneath him. He fell to the ground. An agony of pain shot through his hands. Swiftly he scrambled to his feet, picked up his inanimate burden, and plunged back to the beach. A hut exploded. Its walls blew apart and a ball of black smoke shot upward into the ruddy glow above the trees. A sword of scarlet flame shot skyward in its wake. Flying sparks and bits of burning wood rained down on the priest. His face thrust into the wet cassock wrapped about the prone figure he was carrying, he stumbled and staggered through the choking, blasting heat. Human flesh could not stand this terrific heat. Fire flamed about him. Its heat scorched his lungs. Would he never win through? Oh God!

He must have collapsed momentarily. He had no recollection of leaving the flames behind, but here he was prone on the sand. God, his hands hurt! That fall from the steps. His hands had gone direct into a blazing mass. 'Dolfo? He pulled the cassock from the leper's face. There was still breath in the sick boy.

The house lizard darted across the ceiling. He had missed the mosquito repeatedly. With an all-out effort, he squiggled furiously after the elusive prey. The mosquito flew down into the room. There was a liquid spat as the lizard hit the floor.

Father Conners sat up and looked at the prostrate

lizard. "Got him on the fly that time," he said aloud.
"Break your back?" He touched the lizard with his toe. It
wiggled away. "Nice going." He pulled out his watch.
Totoy and Gracing were both at the village. Frank should
have been back by now. Buff stepped to the front door
and froze in his tracks. A tremendous crimson wash
painted the sky above the village. Billows of surging
smoke shot upward, lanced by demons of roaring red
flame. With one leap he was out of the house. A curious
figure zigzagged toward him. He stopped in mid-stride,
the oncoming figure clearly discernible in the fire's re-
flected light.

"Buff . . . Buff . . ." croaked a hoarse voice, "he's
dying."

A body slipped formlessly to the ground from the
strange creature's arms. Father Connors caught the
speaker by the shoulders. The face was as black as charred
wood. Sweat had run ragged channels through it. Blood-
shot eyes peered out of swollen lids. The brows and lashes
were scorched away. "Frank . . . what's happened . . .
Frank! . . ."

Over the priest's soot-smeared face ran a quiver of pain.
His arms thrust between his legs, he bent over in agony.
Buff's strong hands pulled him erect. "What is it, Frank?
Speak." He jerked his hands into view. "Good God . . .
your hands!"

Father Templeton did not hear him. His whole body
seemed contracted about those quivering pieces of flesh.
He kept moving the hands about, squirming as though
to get away from them. The continuous pain was like
nothing on earth. He had to do something. He had to do
it . . . now, now, before it was too late. He turned and

half stumbled, half ran into the house. Buff leaped after him in swift pursuit. "Wait, wait a moment!" he called.

Father Templeton came plunging out. His oil stocks cupped in his hands. Buff stopped as though shot. Comprehension swiftly flooded him.

"Here, Frank, give me the oils."

Frank backed away. "No. Not this time, Buff," he grated, pain and purpose fighting in his voice. "I've got to do this . . . it's the last time . . . I've got to do it. My hands are no good any more. I heard you. The last thing they do is priest's work . . . priest's hands."

The two hurried to the place where 'Dolfo lay quietly in his last great pain.

Buff stepped forward and Frank stumbled awkwardly to his knees beside the leper. It was not the short form for Extreme Unction, merely on the forehead, that he used. It tore Buff's heart to see the hideous hands twitch with pain as Frank drove them on by sheer strength of will. He slipped to his knees to help him. When the priest came to the anointing of the feet, Buff exposed the leper's bloated legs. Suddenly everything was as clear as day to the white-haired missioner. His eyes were blinking back a strange moisture as they turned to Frank. The grimed and scorched visage was contorting, contracting, quivering with pain, but no trace of disgust, no vestige of fear showed. The voice was tight with repressed pain, but the words came clear. "By this holy unction and His most tender mercy may the Lord forgive you whatever sin you may have committed. . . . Oh, dear God, have mercy. . . . my hands. . . . my hands!"

Buff grabbed for the oil stocks. He was a second too late. Frank Templeton fell across the body of the dead leper.

# Chapter XX

THE light in the binnacle threw its glow on the intent brown face of the youth. His hands flipped the spokes of the wheel a turn or two.

"Juaning, you keep that course till we sight Buenavista Point, eh?" called a voice from the lighted cabin behind him.

"Yes, Captain," he replied without turning.

The light snapped out. There was the creak of the woodwork as the stocky captain eased himself into his bunk. A sigh, a long exhalation of breath. Bed was good after a busy day and Juaning was trustworthy.

Being captain of this little interisland steamer was a dull business. Every week the same thing: Manila to Minandang, the other ports of the Island of Piloan, Santa Cruz the last one, then back to Manila. Next week the same ports, the same people, the same work. One became like the oxen that trotted around in a circle working the crude mills that crushed the sugar cane. Well, he had the Santa Cruz cargo safely abroad. Tomorrow morning there was that special load of copra at Minandang and that would be the last of it. Manila would look good again. And his own shaded veranda . . . the niños . . . the wife. . . . The captain's snores came gently to the helmsman's ears.

The shaded light from the binnacle etched Juaning's young face with deep shadows. Intently he gazed ahead. The night was profoundly dark and still, save for the lulling throb of the engines below decks and the gurgling murmurs of the water as it washed against the ship's side. It was very peaceful, cool. A fine night to sleep. It would be nice to be captain. No need to stand at the wheel all night. Sleep, whenever you wanted to . . . his hands suddenly gripped the spokes of the wheel. The knuckles whitened as he listened, tense, alert for a repetition of the sound. Had he been dreaming? No; there it was again. . . .

The captain came wide awake. The low insistent call came again, "Captain . . . captain!" He lumbered out to the wheel in his pajamas.

"What is it?" he asked sharply.

"Listen . . . you hear? . . . it's there ahead!"

Juaning pointed with one hand into the darkness of the night. A low, carrying, flat tone droned across the water.

"Conch shell," declared the captain, "someone is blowing a conch shell." He scrubbed his scalp with his thick fingers as though to awaken his brain. "Who is it? Pirates?" He shook his head at the stupidity of the idea. Stepping to the edge of the bridge he touched a button. The darkness was cut by a beam of light. He moved the spotlight until it picked up a *banca* almost dead ahead.

"Two to the starboard!" he called out sharply.

"Two to the starboard," echoed Juaning.

The captain spoke into a tube. The engine's steady throbbing diminished, then died away. Under its initial impetus the boat glided on. Through a megaphone the captain hailed the craft.

"Ahoy! Ahoy there!"

"Captain Alvarez! Aho-o-oy!"

"Captain Alvarez," assented the skipper, "Who are you?"

"Manolo . . . stop the ship . . . Manolo."

The captain dropped his megaphone. "Caray!" He ejaculated "Something is wrong. It's Manolo." He called directions down to the engine room. The engines churned briefly in reverse. The boat came to a standstill just as the *banca* drew abreast of it. A sailor came hurrying to the bridge.

"Let down the walk," ordered the captain. The man hastened away while the captain threw on a bathrobe. He directed the spotlight to the walk. Manolo scrambled on deck, and the captain went down to meet him.

"It is the Padre," blurted out Manolo. "Very sick . . . burned."

"Burned?" echoed the captain. "There was a fire?"

Manolo gestured toward the stern of the boat. The captain's face took on a look of utter amazement. A pink flush filled the sky over Santa Cruz. "It is the village," he said in dull wonder.

Manolo nodded. "You will take the Padre to Manila," he ordered. "His hands are burned. He must go to the hospital."

"Of course," assented the captain. He turned toward the bridge and then abruptly wheeled back. "Ai yai, Manolo," he suddenly remembered, "there is a big cargo in Minandang which I must stop for."

"You will not stop. It is important that the Padre get to the doctors at once," insisted Manolo.

"But the office . . . what will the Manila office say if I do not bring them the cargo?"

"The office?" Manolo's voice was heavy with contempt. "What will the office say if the Bishop accuses them of letting the Padre die? Life is more than a cargo of copra."

The captain nodded, still unconvinced. He would have to have more than an ordinary excuse for failing to pick up that cargo. A sick Padre? . . . The office was hard to convince. What would he add to the story?

As though reading his thoughts, Manolo's voice went on. "And you will tell the office," he said, his voice growing cold with hostility, "that you had to do it . . . because I threatened you . . . with a bolo."

The captain was suddenly aware of the tip of Manolo's bolo right at the center of his bathrobe where the belt formed a loose knot.

"Good, good, Manolo," he hastily replied. "That is an excellent excuse."

"And if they send the police after me, I shall send the Archbishop after them."

They stepped to the side of the ship. "He is unconscious," said Manolo. "We will bring him up. Keep the light steady."

Marita, sitting in the bottom of the *banca*, lifted the unconscious priest's head from her lap, while Manolo slipped his hands under the arms. Meanwhile Ramon held the boat steady. Slowly and carefully the trio brought the priest aboard the ship.

"Captain," ordered Manolo, "Ramon and Marita will go with the Padre. Give Marita the medicines you have. She will care for him as far as Manila. I shall pay all when you return."

"Pay?" queried the captain. "There is no pay for this,

Manolo. It is the priest. I am a Catholic also, am I not?"
he protested.

"One that does not go to church on Sundays . . . yes,"
agreed Manolo.

"But there is no church on the ship," protested the
captain.

Manolo shrugged. They were delaying about trifles.
"See that you do not stop at Minandang," he ordered. "If
you forget, then Ramon," he unstrapped his bolo and
gave it to the boy, "will remind you."

He hurried back to his *banca*. The fire in the village
was still his problem.

Ramon brought the ship's medicine chest into the
cabin. Marita's hands were gentle. They swathed the
scorched hands in bandages sopping with cocoanut oil.
The priest was moaning his way back to consciousness.
There were some morphine tablets in the chest. "Swallow,
Padre, swallow," ordered Ramon. He finally managed to
get one of them down the patient's throat. With cotton
the girl tried to remove some of the ravages done by the
fire to the priest's face.

Out of a phantasmagoria of sounds and suffering Father
Templeton came to a momentary dull consciousness.
Something wet hit his face. His eyes opened. The dark
loveliness of Marita's countenance was above him, tears
running unheeded from her eyes. He made a movement
as though to sit up, but Ramon's strong hands held his
shoulders pinned to the berth.

"You must not move, Padre," he insisted gently.

"But . . . but Marita . . ."

"Yes, Padre?" Her face came into his line of vision
again.

"The baby . . . Erning? . . . he is safe?"

A smile broke through her tears. "Yes, Padre. Don Ernesto brought him safely out."

The priest moved his hand. It struck the wall of the bunk, and pain tore through him. His jaws snapped on a shriek.

"Take this tablet, Padre. Take this tablet," ordered Ramon.

Obediently he swallowed the medicine. Moaning, he squirmed about, afraid to turn on his side. He held his hands in the air. Marita's fingers went out to a loose strand of the bandages. He cried aloud. "Do not touch them . . . do not touch them."

Through the long hours they sat with him. Their sympathy reached him even in this nightmare of pain, and he loved them for it. They were near to him. As if he were one of their own. He mumbled something. Marita stooped over him. "It wasn't . . . it wasn't I . . . Don Ernesto saved the child. . . ." His lips slackened as the opiate took effect and he lapsed into a semicomatose condition.

Marita stood up and Ramon folded her in his arms. She cried freely.

"What is it, Chiquita?" he asked softly.

"Oh, he is so good," she sobbed. "The first thing he asked 'is Erning safe?' He did not think of the pain."

"He thinks only of us . . . God will think of him," Ramon consoled her.

"He is so young . . . and good," she tearfully whispered, "and without . . . without his . . ."

Ramon drew her closer to smother the sobs that voiced her fear. Over her shoulder he saw those yellow swathed

hands, tense, upright, symbols of fear and of suffering.
Symbols of prayer to God. The hands of a priest . . . up-
lifted to bless and to save. Ramon could not comfort as
she sobbed again and again "What will he do without his
hands?"

# Chapter XXI

THE clear-cut medicinal odor of antiseptics filled the room. It went with the nature of the room, and was as sharp as the scalpel wielded here to excise corruption, as healing as the skill and devotion that laboured to save.

Antiseptics . . . laving the gleaming steel instruments. Antiseptics . . . dripping from the surgeon's slender hands . . . saving . . . healing . . . a doctor's job . . . a priest's too . . . Christ's hands laid on the brow of sufferers to heal . . . Christ's hands, nailed to the cross . . . to redeem. A man needed hands . . . a voice impinged on his thoughts. He straightened up in his chair, his bandaged hands motionless on the surgical table.

"I won't say they'll be beautiful to look at, Father," said the little Filipino doctor, as his long, thin, skilled fingers unraveled the bandage, "but you will still have them." He paused abruptly. Father Templeton's eyes had suddenly fixed with a tragic intentness on the bandage. "Do you . . . do you think, Father, that . . ."

"Yes," cut in the priest quietly. "Go ahead. I can stand it."

Silently the doctor finished his task. The last strip of bandage fell away. The skin graft had saved the priest's hands.

Slowly Father Templeton turned them. Red, charred

fingers, clawlike, with the long yellowed uncut nails, and across the palms and backs of the hands a sickly staring white band of grafted flesh. He lifted his eyes. "They are not beautiful, Doctor," he agreed in a curiously impersonal voice, "but they will serve."

"That is the main reason why God gave us hands," said the doctor simply, ". . . to serve."

The priest's eyes flicked up suddenly. He had not meant that. Yet, how true it was.

He rose, holding his arms bent, the two hands in front of him. At the door he paused. He was behaving badly. He stepped back into the room. "I still have my hands, Doctor. That is a great deal. If you had not laboured so carefully, so patiently, I would not have them now. I know that. How am I to thank you?" His words were spoken quietly, but his heart looked out of his eyes.

The little doctor went up to him and laid a hand on his arm. "There is no thanks due, Father. I was paying a debt."

"A debt?" The priest groped for the meaning in back of the word. "You mean . . . because I tried to save that . . ."

"Other Filipino," cut in the doctor. "Yes. But not only that. You . . . you . . . well, you are a priest. There are not enough priestly hands in the world."

A curious lump arose in Father Templeton's throat. He dared not risk further conversation. Hastily he turned and followed the nurse from the room.

Back in his room he slumped into a chair and placed his hands on the table. Long he stared at the monstrosities. His mind leaped to the future. The shocked looks when his hands were seen . . . the pitying glance . . . the inevitable question . . . and the unavoidable reply . . . a tin hero . . . rescuing a dying man! Why had all these things happened to him? He had only wanted the peaceful delight of books, the quiet saving of souls through the medium of educating them, teaching them. Life had been rough to him. It had not respected his desires. He had been caught up by its current, whirled into its vortex and now he was cast up on the shore, broken in body, tired in spirit. What was one to do?

He lifted his eyes. A crucifix looked down at him from the wall. A small plaster-cast image on a light-brown wooden cross. Suddenly, with no seeming relevance his mind leaped to that deep, dim night in the church at Santa Cruz when, between the crucifix's nailed palms, a throng of pictures had marshalled themselves before his gaze. The jet of water and the sprawled figure. He had wondered about that. He wondered no longer. It was clear to him now. The leper at the well. It had been the last picture. What was that to indicate? Was this the finish? Or was it a new beginning?

To his ears came the noise of the narrow street outside his window. *Calesa* bells, dust, shouts in Tagalog, Oriental bustle, tropic heat. Manila was a thronging city. His eyes closed and deep in his heart rose a curious nostalgic yearning. It was not for the paved streets of his own city, but for the sea, with its slipping sails and its causeways of sunny gold. Soft sand underfoot and about him the sweetness, the eager life that the flowing arms of Santa Cruz Bay embraced. The fishing fleet in at dawn, the threnody of Magdalen Reef, the long delicious hours of musing in the cove, the sight of Manolo's quiet smile, Totoy's bubbling laugh, mellow lights between the palm trees, and the lilting melody of guitars at night. He wanted just now the breezes from the crests of the waves, million-fingered and soft on his cheeks, not this mordant heat-filled city air.

"Father?"

Startled, he stood up. "Why . . . Father Superior!"

The Superior, accompanied by Father Templeton's physician, walked into the room. "The doctor here informed me that today was the day," he said. "He just told me his work has been successful. I want to be the first to congratulate you." He extended his hand.

Father Templeton looked a trifle bewildered. What was this? Reparation? Congratulations? Or just the introductory to another stiff order. Another push into another maelstrom. His eyes searched the face of his Superior. That white ascetic countenance betrayed nothing. Father Templeton placed his hand in that of the other priest. The Superior made no attempt to clasp it. For a moment he let the hand rest in his palm while a flash of emotion went across his features.

"It will be a while before you are up to a real hand-shake, Father?"

The doctor cut in. "No; not so long. If he works faithfully at the exercises and takes his massage. It all depends on that."

"Well, that is good news." He hesitated. "You are sure he will be able to use them normally, Doctor?"

"Undoubtedly. Their appearance is ruined, but as Father Templeton told me himself, they will serve."

"Thank you, Doctor." The surgeon bowed and quietly left the room. The Superior walked to the window and for a moment seemed to think over a decision. Then turning he said "I'm glad that you still will have the use of your hands, Father. I have felt that this is in great measure my fault."

"Your fault?" gasped Father Templeton. "How can you say that, Father?"

"I sent you to that post. With no intention of excuse I can say that my abruptness in doing so was dictated by the idea that it was what you needed. My intentions were good. My decision was decidedly bad."

"You think because my — my hands are spoiled?"

"No; missionaries don't go by appearances. Our lives are too fundamental to be bothered with such external things as scars. We all have them, as a matter of fact. We don't mind them. You can't expect to fight and come out unmarked. My decision was bad. I thought you a coward — you aren't. You have more stuff than I have."

Father Templeton's knees felt curiously weak. He sat down suddenly in his chair. Sweeter words he had never heard. "Are you just saying this to make me feel good?" he asked trying hard to keep a tremour out of his voice.

The level gaze of the older priest met his. "I'm not that sort of person," was his direct response. "I'm saying it because I mean it." There was no doubting the man's stern honesty. "You really did not belong out here. Your temperament and inclination were not the kind for a missioner. It was unjust of us to expect as much from you as the others." He paused and drew a deep breath. "And while we realize that your work in Santa Cruz has been good and this . . . this last occurrence heroic, it would not be fair to shackle you to that sort of existence."

The glad light suddenly died out of Father Templeton's eyes. The words of praise had been sweet indeed, and had sent the blood surging through him as never before in his life. His efforts were officially acknowledged. And now he knew what he faced. He read it in the eyes that stared at him so impersonally across the table. Another appointment. He had ruined himself in a heroic attempt. The heroism was acknowledged but there was still work to do. Work! He was tired of it. Solitude. Quiet. Books. Prayer. This was what he wanted. His own people again.

The Superior began to speak again. Slowly, remorselessly, the words came and from down the hospital's dim broad corridors the sound of a closing door reached the young priest's ears.

The *calesa* idled down the narrow street. The horses' hoofs clip-clopped rhythmically. Trot . . . run . . . clip-clop . . . trot . . . run . . . clip-clop . . . trot . . . run clippety-clop . . . till the day is done . . . clippety-clop, clippety-clop. The dark-faced *cochero* was lulled with the melody of it. A hissed sound brought him erect. A white-cassocked figure beckoned. A Padre! He brought the pony awake and drew the conveyance smartly to the curb. His right hand whipped out the curved wicker shield that went over the wheel so the passenger would not soil his garments on entering. He held the horse steady. There was no billowing motion of the *calesa* as the passenger entered. He looked at the Padre. "You want to ride, Padre?"

"Yes, but you must help me in. I . . . I cannot use my hands."

"How, Padre?"

"My hands." He held up the white-gloved members.

"Oh . . ." The *cochero* dropped the reins, wiped a pair of dirty broken-nailed hands on his trousers, leaned over and took the priest by the arm. Carefully he helped him in. "Where to, Padre?"

"Where to?"

"Yes. Where do you want to go?"

Where did he want to go? Any place. Away from the confining walls of that hospital room. To think . . . think . . . and decide. He was hurt. Curious how the fulfillment of that which one wants brings with it pain. Or did he want it? Maybe he only thought he did.

"Padre?" The *cochero* had screwed around in his seat.

"O, yes. The Luneta."

The *cochero* clucked and rattled his whip on the top of the cab. Briskly the horse stepped out. The *cochero* slumped sidewise.

"You just come from the hospital, Padre. Did you break the hands?"

"No, I burnt them."

"Burnt? Ai yai! Berry painful that." He pulled up a trouser leg. "I get burnt once." He showed the scars on his leg. "It is not like the bolo cut. That hurts only when I move. The burn hurts all the time."

They left the Walled City and mingled with the traffic on stately Taft Avenue.

"How you burn the hands?"

"There was a fire in my village. It was not here in Luzon but in Piloan."

"Piloan? I have relatives there. You know Santa Cruz?"

"That is where I am from," said the priest suddenly interested. "Who are your relatives?"

"Antonio Barredo. He is my cousin."

"Why, I know him well."

Into his mind flashed a picture of the cockpit at Santa Cruz. Antonio and Evaristo; Evaristo and his final threat to return, his last vindictive look. He had not given it much thought. Strange that it should crop up now, to add its disturbance to the difficulty of the decision he had to make. For, in a curiously psychic way, he felt certain that some day Evaristo would return to Santa Cruz.

They came to the Luneta. The *cochero* helped him to descend. "How much must I pay you?"

"It is nothing, Padre," refused the man.

"What? You are not going to charge me?"

The man shook his head in refusal. The priest understood then that he was being treated as a friend; as the parish priest of the man's relatives. "Now listen, chico, you take the money or I will tell 'Tonio that you do not do what I tell you. Come here and get that money out of my pocket."

Reluctantly the *cochero* obeyed. He plunged his hand into the priest's pocket and fumbled around for the coins. Suddenly he laughed aloud.

"What are you laughing at?"

"I think, Padre . . . if the policeman comes he will think I am stealing from the Padre and pok! into the calabozo I go."

Father Templeton could not help smiling. "Take a peseta for the ride and a peseta for some pansit."

"It is too much," protested the man.

But the priest would have no refusal. The *calesa* drifted away.

Past the Legaspi-Urdaneta monument Father Templeton strolled. He glanced aloft at the two gallant figures.

The cross and the sword. "Dios, Honor y Rey." Their motto. Valiant men, heroic missioners. He realized that he belonged to a royal lineage. He was carrying on the work those gallant men had inaugurated.

Manila's Luneta is a delightful spot. Father Templeton wanted to think. The wide green lawns, the tremendous bay before him, this was what he needed. His head was still filled with the words spoken that day to him by the Superior. He found a bench and sat down facing Manila Bay. The sun was on the point of setting. His hands, gloved in white cotton, he placed in his lap. A grimness came about his mouth as he looked at them. They were now things to keep hidden. For some time he sat immobile. His mind swept clean of all thought, absorbing the sweetness and fulness of the sea, the sky, and the sunset.

He had flung his energy of thought, strength, and prayerful striving into a definite task. Small had been the achievement. Out of it he came, torn and tired. The world wagged on. His herculean effort had been a mere wave smashed to foam on an unyielding rock. All that remained to him was the peace of spent effort. That was all. The guerdon of effort is in the energy expended — what a cynical thought! It would not be the attitude of Manolo or his people. Well, wide vistas beget men of wide vision. His people lived with the ocean for a floor and the sky for a ceiling. They could not be small. Simple they were. Greatness is simple. Depth and breadth are simple. Life's philosophy for them was beautiful and simple and profound. Battle the waves for a living. The Designer of their house had fitted it with all their requirements for body and soul — food, beauty, health. Their lives were as the tides. Running in with joy, going out with mournful sadness. Not the sadness of grief but reluctance that the strife is so swiftly over. Their life is a tide and the tides of the world are in His hands.

The priest shook himself and stood up. He had been doing a lot of woolgathering. Strangely, it brought comfort, like those idle hours at home on the beach at Santa Cruz Bay. He looked at his gloved hands. He knew now the work and the price of it. The decision was his. But no, he had made the decision weeks ago. He had felt for one brief moment the strength of a Divine Hand upholding him. He knew now that the Power on which he was learning to rely would be with him always. And he smiled as he remembered the Master's words, "O, ye of little faith, why did you doubt?"

Unconsciously, he had lifted his hands. He gazed at them a moment. Then, very slowly, he tore away the gloves and dropped them in the sea.

# FULFILLMENT:

"They enclosed a great number of fishes;
but their net was breaking."

# Chapter XXII

## 1

THE incoming boat was as yet a distant wisp of smoke as the longshoremen watched its progress. They were squatting on the end of the pier waiting for the boat's arrival.

"Gracing?" said one.

"Good morning," replied the roly-poly fiscal. His voice was not affable. "The boat?"

The longshoreman flicked his eyebrows toward the bay. Gracing pushed his kalugong back from his brow and squinted. His eyes were not good for distances.

"You got a box on the boat?" asked the longshoreman, with an eye to possible business.

"No."

The other longshoreman had a try. "Maybe there is a visitor from Manila? Eh?"

"Not for me."

"A Padre? eh?" opined the first shrewdly.

Gracing grunted assent. He did not want to speak about the matter. He felt surly. It was not part of his duty to meet people at the pier. The houseboy could do that. The longshoremen were quite aware of that, and their curiosity was evidence of the fact.

"There is a new Padre," Gracing said.

"A new one?"

"Caray!" ejaculated the other. "The other one — the Americano — he is dead."

"No, loco, he is not dead."

"Then why does he not come back?"

Gracing did not reply. It was a question he had asked himself repeatedly. One of the longshoremen spat speculatively at a barnacle-crusted post in the water. "Maybe he does not like the Filipinos."

Gracing's face grew a trifle pink. These ignorant ones could not see a mountain if it were against their noses. "That is right. He does not like the Filipinos." His tones grew acid. "So he roasts his hands like a *lechon* to save one."

The longshoreman pulled at the brim of his long hat, for it was plain that the Jellyfish had not slept well last night. He spat philosophically into the water, and would have liked to make a retort. But one had to be careful with this fat fellow.

"Then you will have a new Padre?" he ventured pacifically.

"Have I not said it already?"

His interlocutor gave it up as a bad job. Rising to his feet, he went to a group of people who had just arrived and vainly tried to assist them with their baggage.

The ship was in plain sight. It rapidly drew nearer. Gracing thrust his hands into his pockets and waited. One of the longshoremen began to coil a rope.

"This new one . . . what is his name?"

Gracing looked at him. He was respectful. "Padre Brown."

"He is big?"

"How should I know?"

"He will have a satchel?"

"Of course, carabao face!" retorted Gracing angrily. "You think the Padre has only the shirt on his back."

"You will carry the satchel to the convento?" asked the man.

"No, I will not," retorted Gracing in a loud voice. "Am I the fiscal or am I a longshoreman?"

"You are the fiscal, Gracing, and I am a longshoreman. So I will carry his satchel . . . for twenty-five centavos."

"What! Twenty-five centavos!"

"If there are two, it will be fifty centavos."

"You think I am from the mountains? Fifteen centavos for one and forty centavos, if two."

They fell to haggling. The price was finally set at Gracing's figure. The exchange had relieved some of Gracing's pent-up feelings. With a less gloomy eye he watched the boat slowly warp in. Alertly he scanned the passengers as they jostled down the gangplank. No sign of a cassock appeared. The longshoreman had picked up a customer. He was torn two ways. "The Padre, where is he?" he asked.

"Asleep or seasick, I suppose," came Gracing's disgusted reply.

"I cannot wait, Gracing," said the longshoreman, "there is this box here. . . ."

"Go take your box!"

The longshoreman hastened away.

"Now I must go and find him, and carry his satchel too." It boded ill for the new Padre as Gracing shuffled up the gangplank.

2

The sound of a siren came faintly, its hoarse tone softened by the distance. It was just entering the bay. Father Conners, pacing the veranda, heard it. He knew its meaning. For the village it was the glad herald of the boat's weekly arrival, but for him it was the sad wail of defeat. His brow clouded. The "Buffalo" had bucked through so many obstacles victoriously that the taste of defeat was bitter. It was like the tart taste of medicine to the tongue of one who has always been well. Well, maybe it was a medicine. His pride needed this dose. A setback was good for a man. It kept him aware of the fact that he was not God Almighty. Sheer determination, deep thought, persistent prayer were not infallible means to achieve success.

He drew from his cassock the note that had reached him yesterday. The Superior's firm neat hand had carried many a bit of unwelcome news to him, but none that he had disliked as much as this. The offending paragraph he read again.

"I should have granted his request to go home long ago. It is my opinion that we erred here. He has the will to make efforts, heroic efforts. It would be unjust and cruel to ask more of him. He is marred for life. At least let him spend the years to come in congenial occupation with no fear of even more drastic incidents to face. I am going to Manila to arrange for his departure. Father Brown will arrive on the Tuesday boat to take over. Please meet him and assist him to get settled as the new missioner for Santa Cruz."

Buff stalked inside the house, tore the letter with strong, violent hands, and flung it in a basket. He looked about him. The books had gathered dust these past weeks. He called Totoy.

"Get a case and pack Father Templeton's books," he ordered. Totoy's mouth dropped open. "He is not coming back?"

"No." The unusual curtness of the reply held the boy silent for a moment.

"He is too sick?" he asked anxiously.

"That isn't the reason," replied the priest irritably. "He is going home . . . to America."

Totoy's eyes grew wide. A catastrophe had befallen him. Silently he left the room, a stricken look on his face.

Buff went back to the veranda and resumed his pacing. His efforts had failed. And he had felt so sure of the outcome. A man could never be sure of what his efforts might bring. To his mind, Father Templeton had finally found himself. Now was the time for him to launch forth really into the work. Instead, came this dogmatic decision of the Superior . . . wrecking everything. His weeks and months of advice and direction were all wasted. Well, failure was the everyday portion of the missioner. It hurt so much, though, when it was the matter of a brother priest.

Louder to his ears came the sound of the siren. The boat was in. He jammed his sun helmet on his head and strode out of the convento down the white coral roadway. Abreast of the village he stopped to look at the gaps in the thick clustering palms where the fire had claimed tribute. Sounds of ax and hammer mingling with the cheery call of workmen came to his ears. The village was rebuilding rapidly and Don Ernesto was the fairy godfather. If only Frank could have seen this. Abruptly he banished the thought. Father Templeton's association with Santa Cruz was a closed chapter.

Soon his swift stride was kicking up the fine dust that carpeted the narrow road between the *tiendas*. He lifted his head and stopped in his tracks as he saw advancing to meet him a familiar figure. There was no mistaking that slim white form. For a moment Buff's hopes soared high and then, as abruptly, fell dead. The Superior's words had been too explicit. He would just be returning for his beloved books and a word of farewell. And then he caught sight of Gracing. A curious Gracing. A Gracing he had never seen before. In his pudgy hands he clasped two huge satchels. With a bound, Buff cleared the intervening space.

"Frank!" he ejaculated and he had him by both shoulders.

Father Templeton looked at him with shining eyes. No words were needed.

"I talked Father Superior into giving Father Brown another appointment," he finally managed to say.

"You scamp!" roared Buff.

A Chino peered out of his *tienda*. "Sus Maria Sep!" he piously ejaculated and slopped forward on his slippers through the dust to give the priest a series of exuberant kowtows. Heads bobbed into view around posts, trees, *tienda* doors; people shuffled out, and in that curiously Oriental way, a crowd metamorphosed out of thin air. Greetings, bows innumerable. They marched down the road along with the two priests.

"Do you have a lot of people to meet you when you come home?"

Father Templeton looked up at this strange question. Buff Conners' face was wrinkled in a wonderful smile and suddenly he remembered. It was the question he had put to him months ago.

"I don't know what has happened," he said happily.

"I do, my fine lad. You're coming home. That's what has happened," was the robust assurance.

Two longshoremen kept importuning Gracing for the privilege of carrying the Padre's satchels. But the fiscal was obdurate in spite of perspiration and audible gruntings at the unusual efforts.

"What's that ahead?" queried Father Templeton suddenly as they came almost abreast of the village where the work on the new buildings was being done.

"Looks like another reception committee," replied Father Conners, gazing at the motley group, tools in hand, that blocked the roadway.

"Ap-o-o!" came a long welcoming cry from a figure in front of them. Eagerly he came forward, right-hand palm extended. It was Manolo. Father Templeton quietly placed his right hand, palm down, upon it. Manolo went down on his right knee and lifted the priest's hand to his lips. It was only then that Buff noticed the monstrosity. The burn-scarred fingers, the leprous white patch of skin graft upon the back of the hand. Father Templeton's eyes were intent upon Manolo as he rose. There was no sign of repugnance in the *Capitán's* face. He rose still holding the hand.

"The burns were very bad, Apo?" he said.

"It doesn't hurt any more, Manolo," was the simple reply and their eyes met in a glance of deep understanding. The wall that had stood between them was demolished. The village had accepted the priest unreservedly. He was one of them now.

"I owe you a thank you, Manolo, from the heart," said the priest quietly, "for stopping the boat that night." Manolo grinned.

"It was nothing, Apo. The captain was worried about the cargo from Mindanang, but I persuaded him our cargo was more important," and he laughed as he began to recount the story and the persuasiveness of a bolo held at the right angle.

As they drew near the convento a loud "Hola! Hola!" caused everyone to stop. A shirt-sleeved figure carrying a child was hastening to intercept them.

"It is Don Ernesto," said Manolo happily.

It was a new Don Ernesto. Down he went on his knee to kiss the priest's hand and then he stood up to display his grandchild. "I went back to get Erning to greet you too, Padre," he said, his face beaming. "Does he look like me?" he added.

"Well," said Father Templeton, his face transfigured with joy at a regained friend, "I can tell you better when he has a moustache."

A roar of laughter greeted his sally.

"Padre, tomorrow night there will be a *Bienvenida* at the Casa Grande for you," Don Ernesto hastened to declare. "All the village will be there. Everyone. Also you, Padre Conners?"

"Also I," assented Buff heartily.

The crowd was shooed away by Don Ernesto. Preparations must start at once. He called everyone by name and began giving orders right and left.

The door of the convento burst open. A startled Totoy

dashed for the stairs, missed his step, and landed in a heap at the feet of Father Conners. He swung him quickly upright.

"Are you hurt, 'Toy?" asked Father Templeton anxiously.

"I am happy, Faddaire," was the astonishing reply.

"He sure is," commented Buff, "deliriously so."

Father Templeton made for the steps, but the boy dashed in ahead of him. "Do not come in," he called from the top of the steps, "only do not come in, Faddaire."

"All right, 'Toy," said Buff. "Go ahead; we'll wait." He turned to Father Templeton. "He wants to get your books back in their shelves. Everything must be just as you left it."

Father Templeton's answering smile was suddenly erased by a sepulchral greeting at his elbow. He spun about to face Lacay Luis. The crowd grew silent as the sage greeted the priest. He cleared his throat. "Today I have seen two wonders," he began, "the return of our Padre — " a curious warmth went through Father Templeton at the phrase — "and Gracing carrying another's burden." A disarming smile accompanied the latter statement.

Gracing, perspiring, mumbled, "Tomorrow will be a greater wonder if I am not as stiff as you are after carrying these two hundred kilos of satchels."

Lacay Luis shuffled over to him and put his wrinkled hand familiarly on Gracing's shoulder. "He who eats pepper gets a burnt tongue."

They all laughed, Gracing included. The priests entered the house; they could hear the two men talking about the *Bienvenida* and just what they were going to eat.

As though by common consent, both priests made for the veranda. Totoy had just drawn up the *mañana* chairs. Father Templeton handed him his sun helmet.

"Ai yai!" exclaimed the boy, noticing the priest's hands. "It is berry painful, Faddaire?"

"Oh, no," smiled the priest.

"You cannot move them?"

"Not very well. But I can move them," and he demonstrated.

"I will put cocoanut oil on them every day, Faddaire," volunteered the boy. "It is berry good for that."

Father Templeton gravely agreed while Father Conners grinned. "He's bound to make you as good as new," he said.

Buff swiftly launched into an account of what had happened since Father Templeton's departure. 'Dolfo, the leper, had been buried at Don Ernesto's expense. The latter had shown a complete change of heart toward his son. In fact, Ramon and Marita lived with him now at the Casa Grande. Fortunate it was, too, for the people needed his aid as never before in order to rebuild their fire-gutted village. "You must have talked to him like a Dutch uncle," opined Buff with a gleam in his eye. "It certainly has cured him of his one failing."

"It was one of the hardest things I had to do," said Father Templeton slowly. "I don't make friends easily. Losing one is like losing a part of myself. But your words, that night I asked your advice, made my duty clear to me. I don't remember much of what I told Don Ernesto that eventful night. It was not pleasant. It was the truth as I saw it."

"You were not afraid, Frank?"

"Well, Buff, that's the strangest thing. You know, I don't think that I'll ever be afraid again. I've learned something that is going to take away a lot of the hardships of a missioner's life. Something I find it hard to talk about."

Father Conners did not reply, for there was nothing for him to say. The two men sat silently, looking out to sea.

"You know, Buff, I think you understand."

"Yes, Frank, the knowledge you have been given is a rare thing. See that you never forget it."

The moon flooded the bay with its silver radiance. The palm leaves glinted like blades of silver in its splendour. Father Templeton stepped quietly from the soft light into the church's entrance. His heart was full with the gladness of this homecoming. The deep peace of the darkness reached out to him like a blessing.

With a curious flash of remembrance, his mind leaped back to the shadowed portals of Minandang's church and the huddled beggar. It had all started from that. His eyes turned, and suddenly a shiver went through him. A huddled figure was on the floor. Were his eyes playing tricks on him? The figure rose and drew near.

"Padre?" said a low hoarse voice.

The priest stepped back in alarm.

"Evaristo!" he exclaimed.

"Yes. I have been waiting here. I know you used to come here every night — to pray."

"You — you want something of me?"

"Yes."

"What is it?"

"Your forgiveness."

"You mean for that trouble — in the cockpit?"

"Yes, Padre."

"You have that freely, Evaristo. You were excited that day and did not mean all the things you said," condoned the priest.

The priest exhaled an audible sigh of relief. In the dim light he glimpsed the man's outstretched hand, suppliant, seeking. It came home to him with startling clarity that this was the way of human hands and would be their endless way . . . some outstretched to receive, others to give. He placed his own newly healed hand in that of Evaristo. "What is past, is past, Evaristo . . . forgiven and forgotten."

"Thank you, Padre. I will be better from now on," he promised. "If I can do anything for you at any time, you must let me know. I owe you very much."

"You do not owe me anything, Evaristo," assured the priest, "but I will be glad of your help."

"I owe you nothing?" queried the bowed man. "How can you say that?"

The priest peered at him, amazed by the intense feeling in the man's voice.

"Rodolfo was my youngest brother," he said simply.

Rodolfo — the leper whom he had cared for — Evaristo's brother! The man's lips found the priest's hand. "Good night, Padre."

A leper had begun this work of his initiation into the inner mysteries of God's love. Another leper had continued the lesson. Thoughtfully, he made his way into the church and knelt before the crucifix. The words of thanksgiving came easily, for he was home again and among his own people. It had been a wonderful day, a day full of comfort, comfort pressed down and shaken together and running over.

He rose and walked back to the convento. Yes, it was good to be home, good to know that he was back on his job. Looking out across the quiet waters of the sea, he knew that he would never know storm or stress in his soul again. Difficulties would come, of course; and sorrow and suffering and loss. But against them all there was the thought of Him who had told His followers what to expect in their service of Him. "And I shall ask the Father, and He shall send you another Comforter. . . ."